Ruthless Bachelor
Reana Malori

CONTENTS

Ruthless Bachelor
Summary

People say I don't have a heart...or a soul. That I'm not capable of caring about anyone but myself. They're wrong. I love my family, even my troublemaker little brother. Women? Meh, not so much. I learned the hard way to never confuse my heart with my dic... well, you get it.

I have the perfect life. I answer to no one and everything I do is on my terms. Nothing gets in the way of what I want, and yes, that includes women. I've had countless attractive women in my bed, for a night, but never more than that.

Heads up ladies, I have very special skills that women crave, but I'm a one and done with you kinda guy. Don't give me your number. I won't be calling you. Names are optional. I'll probably forget it anyway. I'm not a complete ass about it. I always make sure to have a car waiting in the morning.

And then Anya walks into my neat, compartmentalized life and now the jokes on me. One taste of her, and I want more. Need more. Crave more. Does Anya really believe that she can deny me? Hasn't anyone told her that I play dirty? I'm not going anywhere because I know I have what she can't resist. One problem, she seems to hold the same power over me. My name is Hunter, but I might just have become the prey.

One
Hunter

Sipping my favorite scotch, I looked around at all the single women mixing and mingling, playing their nightly game of 'Catch a Bachelor.' If only these women knew the truth, they'd probably run for the front door as fast as they could. I could describe every single man in this room as an Apex Predator, myself included. We didn't play fair. We played to win. And tonight, winning the game meant getting the hottest, most beautiful woman in the room to take a ride in the elevator upstairs to our expensive apartment.

Just thinking about the possibilities in store for tonight brought a smile to my face. I took another sip and watched as one of my buddies strolled through the crowd, making his way over to me. A half-smile tilted my lips as I watched him get closer.

"Hunter," he greeted, sitting in the chair across from me.

"Bryce," I returned, lifting my glass in a mock toast.

His gaze flitted around the packed room of people before he turned back to me. "Full house tonight."

"Yup," I agreed. This bar was the place to be. The luxury could not be hidden or denied. Living here was the ultimate sign of success, and I deserved every bit of the life I'd created for myself.

"Yeah, this place is a damn smorgasbord of beautiful women," he said, winking at a woman walking past us. "Plus, you know how it is in here when the sun goes down. The food isn't the only buffet laid out for us to sate our appetite. It's been a long ass week, and I'm ready for some fun."

Usually, I agreed with him, but I was feeling off-kilter this evening. There was something in the air, and I wasn't sure how to explain it. "I'm not even sure why I'm down here tonight. It's been a long fucking week. I just want to relax, not deal with this game." I could feel a headache growing behind my eyes. I'd been in the middle of negotiations for two weeks working on a purchase from a small information technology company. They had software I needed to expand my business to better support my federal government clients. This deal could not fail. If it did, there would be significant ramifications for my company.

Pinching my fingers against my temple, I tried to hold off the pain making its way through my head. The company knew they had me over a barrel because my Chief Technology Officer let it slip that our government contracts were as good as dead without their software. I might just fire his ass on Monday.

Now, because of his fuck-up, I had to come up with a new strategy to help the owners understand this wasn't a deal they should pass up. I'd offered them a sweet deal, but they needed to get on board.

My fist clenched as I thought of my CTO's fuckup. It would serve his ass right if I made a few calls and made sure he never worked in the northeast again. My anger and frustration at his reckless slip of the tongue wasn't going away anytime soon. I needed something to take the edge off. Maybe I needed to take a page from Bryce's playbook and get lost between the legs of a buxom blonde or brunette.

Bryce lifted his feet and placed them on the table in front of him. Rude? Yes. Then again, it wasn't my building. If there was a problem with what he was doing, someone would speak up. Then again, with how much we paid to live here, maybe they wouldn't.

"Did you wrap up that acquisition?" He asked, his gaze tracking the women around the room, trying to identify his prey for the night.

Shaking my head, I placed my drink on the table beside me before leaning forward. "No. I have a feeling I'm going to spend more on this deal than I thought." And just the thought of that frustrated me even more.

"Is it too late to walk away?"

There was no easy answer to that question. On the one hand, I wanted to wash my hands of this whole thing. Contracts with the government always came with a load of bullshit extras. Picking up my drink and taking another sip, I felt the burn down my throat and let it calm the fire inside me.

"At this point, I wish I could. There's some real momentum behind what they're doing with their software. This is a game changer for me." I shook my head. "No. It's too late to walk away." I could feel my jaw clenching. "This shit was supposed to wrap up two days ago. If I don't get what the fuck I want, heads are gonna roll."

"Damn, man. What are you going to do?"

Leaning back in my seat, I reached over and picked up my drink before answering. "I'm going to win. That's what I do. There's no other option."

Laughing, Bryce nodded. "Yes. Yes, winning is definitely what you do. Just don't ruin anyone's life in the process."

I glared at him. "What the fuck are you talking about?" I knew, but I wondered if he was brave enough to say it.

"As if you didn't know that your name on the street is the Grim Reaper. Try that 'I don't know what you're talking about' shit with someone else. You don't have to upend someone's entire life just because you want what they have." He took another sip of his drink as he stared at me, his eyes crinkling at the corners.

"Asshole," I gritted out, which made him chuckle.

"Right back at you. Now," Bryce exclaimed, finally removing his feet from the table, "what kind of trouble are we getting into tonight?"

"I'm not seeing anyone worth the trouble," I respond.

Here's a bit of truth serum from me, which I know isn't always well received. I don't do well with people looking to latch on to someone who can help them get a leg up in this world. No, don't take that the wrong way.

I'm not saying people don't deserve to get rewarded for hard work, dedication, loyalty, or any other word you can add to the mix. On the other hand, I distance myself from people who appear needy and desperate. Their only focus on life is to latch on to someone else and ride their coattails. Those are the kind of people I walk away from as fast as I can.

Here's the thing: if you can't make it on your own, then I don't want you around me. That's not my game and I can do without the trouble. My little brother, Caleb, tells me I have a fucked-up view of people. Yeah, maybe I do. Then again, he and I grew up in a family dynamic as fucked up as any sob story. Our father was a mean drunk and regularly abused our mother. Our mother was a saint. She deserved so much more than the life she had with our father, taking his abuse for too many years to count. Even though she was hurting and struggling to deal with the pain he put her through, she tried to instill the right morals and values into Caleb and me. Ones like kindness, charity, empathy. All the things that made a person weak and prone to manipulation.

Thank God neither my brother nor I followed that path.

Bryce's voice broke through my inner musings. "I see we have some new visitors to the Tower." His eyes were focused on the entrance to the large bar area.

A little about this place, which we fondly referred to as the Bachelor Tower. This place caters to men. Single men. Wealthy Men. No kids. No women. No animals. Well, women and animals were allowed if a resident escorted them.

This place was meant for us. It was all ours, and it was perfect. We had a lounge/bar that served the best scotch, whiskey, or whatever you preferred to drink. It also had a fully equipped gym, a sauna to release the tension, and yes... even a cigar lounge for those who occasionally enjoyed a good toke after a long day closing multi-million-dollar deals.

Safe haven didn't even begin to explain the feeling of this place. It was so much more than that.

The one exception to the no-woman rule was the bar. Women could come and go as they pleased, but they could not go beyond these walls without an escort. It was a hard and fast rule of the Tower. And as far as I know, everyone abided. There'd been talk of allowing women to live here, but from what I'd heard, that hadn't gone over very well. Hell, the only reason I had my apartment here was because my mentor had it first. When he found a woman to marry, he moved out. I was the first person he called about moving in. It was all hush-hush since getting into this place was like getting entry into a secret society. An invitation to move into Bachelor Tower was almost invaluable.

But, hell, I wasn't looking a gift horse in the mouth, but I also knew without my mentor, they wouldn't have let me within thirty feet of the front door. Didn't matter how much money I had in my bank account. To move into the Tower, there are extensive background checks. And let's just say, my background ain't squeaky clean. In fact, it's pretty much black and gray from some of the shit I've done in my past and the people who helped me get a leg up.

See, I know what it's like to be at the bottom, but my pride and ego wouldn't let me stay there.

Turning my gaze to where Bryce was looking, my eyes homed in on the vision in front of me, and everything around me stopped. Including the breath in my lungs. My drink was halfway to my mouth when my hand paused. I couldn't take my eyes off her.

Goddamn, she was beautiful. This was one woman I definitely wanted to know better.

Laughter met my ears, but I didn't turn to look at Bryce. "You can't have her," he said. His tone was light, but I wasn't in a playing mood. "I saw her first, and I plan on doing bad things with her all night."

"I can't have who?" Even I could hear the deadly growl in my voice. I don't know why I felt a surge of jealousy as I looked at the woman walking with her friend. If Bryce thought he would push me out of the way and stop me from getting what I wanted, he'd better think again.

"The blonde, of course."

My head whipped around. "Of course?" I couldn't help but question his words. Did he miss the stunning creature walking next to the blonde? Legs a mile long. Body like a country back road. Wavy hair hung down her back. Full, lush lips. Nah, I didn't want the blonde. Watching her walk closer to me, well, closer to the bar, I knew my night had just gotten much more interesting.

Bryce opened his big mouth again. "Yeah, you need to find your own woman tonight."

I ignored Bryce and his inconsequential words. That he'd passed over and dismissed the beauty walking next to the blonde was unfortunate. Then again, his preference wasn't my concern. My gaze tracked her every move. I watched her smile at the bartender as he took her drink order. My pants tightened at the thought of having her beneath me. Yeah, things were beginning to look up in my world.

Calling over a waiter walking by, I told him what I wanted. He nodded and walked off to take care of my request.

"What did you just do?" Bryce asked, a frown on his face.

"Don't worry about me. You can have your chosen woman. She doesn't entice me in the least. I have... someone else who's caught my attention." Tipping my drink at my friend, I stared across the room as things played out. If everything went according to plan, I would have an exceptionally good night.

Two
Anya

"Why are we here, Carrie?" Looking around the bar filled with handsome as hell men and beautiful, thin women, I couldn't help thinking I looked frumpy and out of place. This wasn't my style, yet here I was.

My friend rolled her eyes at me, something she'd been doing since she came to my house earlier tonight. "Because you need to get out of the house. You never have any fun. We need this night out, Anya."

I sighed, adjusting the black sheath dress I'd managed to squeeze into for the night.

Usually, no matter what night it was, you'd find me sitting on my couch with a bowl of ice cream. My three-year-old son, Malachi, would be cuddled next to me. Once Carrie had proven she would not take no for an answer, I'd gotten lucky. My parents had agreed to watch Malachi for the weekend so I could come out and have a little fun. I mean, it's not like I really needed to come out for any reason, but Carrie was like a damn tornado. "No, I don't. I like my quiet nights inside."

"No, you do not. That's a dang lie and you know it," Carrie snarked at me. "You've convinced yourself of that because you think it's what you should do. It's the responsible thing to do because you're a single mom. But everyone deserves to have fun." Pausing at the door to the infamous Bachelor Tower, she turned to me. "Promise me you'll try to let loose and have a good time."

Smiling at my friend, I shook my body as if preparing to get in the ring with a heavyweight boxer. "Fine. I got this. Don't worry about me. I have left Mommy Anya behind. Tonight, is all about Sex Kitten Anya. I'm gonna find me a man with a big dic—" I paused as other people walked by us. The men had smiles on their faces and a gleam in their eyes. The women, well, let's just say they must have sucked on a lemon because their faces were all scrunched up in distaste. Well, whatever. In for a penny, in for a pound. "…a big dick and have him blow my back out."

Carrie laughed and I joined in with her. This was the first time in a long time that we had a night like this. We first met in college when assigned to the same dorm room. We were a mismatched pair—a blonde beauty from Tuscaloosa, Alabama, and the mouthy girl from Alexandria, Virginia, with too many curves and not enough self-esteem. No one expected us to become so close. Not even the two of us. But something about us clicked. We discovered we were the same person, just in two different bodies.

Now, with almost ten years, one amazing little boy, one failed marriage, and many ups and downs between us, we were still as close as ever. When she moved to Boston, Massachusetts, for a job at a law firm, she asked me to come with her. After six months, I did. Within two years, she was divorced and recovering, while I raised my beautiful son all on my own. His father wasn't in the picture, which was fine with me. He paid child support, which I placed in a college fund, and stayed away from our son. Looking back, I should have known he was too good to be true, but his good looks and slick words had blinded me.

Grabbing Carrie's hand, I walked up to the doorman, who let us in after confirming that we were only allowed in the bar, that elevator access was restricted, and that we could not roam through the Tower without an escort from a resident.

The closer we got to the bar entrance, the louder the conversation within the space grew. It wasn't obnoxious or overly loud, but it was the sound of steady conversation. The clink of glasses. The soft giggles of women. My brief spurt of bravery left me, and my feet planted on the ground.

"Carrie, are you sure we should be here? This isn't our normal scene. I mean, they had to give us rules before we were allowed into the lobby. I'm not cut out for this." I moved to turn around when she grabbed me around the waist and twisted me until I was facing the bar entrance.

"Come on, Anya. You promised. Now, if you don't get your butt in there, I'm gonna make an ugly scene. You don't want that, but I'm getting desperate." She stood in front of me with a pout on her lips. "I need this, and so do you. It's been over six months since I got out of the house and did something just for me. You need this night out just as much as I do. Stop fighting it. Give it thirty minutes. If you still want to leave after that, we will." She glanced away from me and bit at her trembling lip. I felt my heart clench. I knew what my best friend had been going through this past year. Her ex-husband had really done a number on her self-confidence. She turned back to me and stood a little taller. "Come on, Anya. Do this for me. Okay?" At my nod, she smiled big. "Okay, so stop pussyfooting around, girl. Let's go."

I couldn't help but laugh. "Did you just tell me to stop pussyfooting around? Who even uses that term anymore?" At her laugh, we grabbed each other's arms and marched into the room. She was right. Netflix and ice cream could wait another day.

The ambiance inside the bar was breathtaking. Men in three-piece suits mingled with men in polo shirts and blue jeans. The women were dressed to the nine's and looked glamorous. Half of them could be models if they chose. Taking stock of my own dress, I knew my lack of wealth was visible for all to see, but I didn't care. I was here to have fun, have some drinks, and enjoy a night away from being a mommy.

Scanning the space, I noticed a man watching me from across the room. Blond. Black suit. Forest green shirt. No tie. Big hands. How do I know he has big hands? Because one was holding a glass with an amber liquor inside. I wonder if his feet matched. I smiled at the thought because clearly, I was already thinking about the possibilities.

"Let's head to the bar," Carrie called out before walking in that direction.

"Sure," I mumbled, following behind her. I wanted to turn and look at the guy sitting in the chair across the room, but I didn't want to appear too eager. I had to play it cool, right?

Okay, just breathe, Anya. Don't trip over your own feet and face plant in the middle of one of the most exclusive places in Boston. Just breathe. Stop being foolish. Was my skirt riding up? Did I wear the right panties? Please don't let me have lipstick on my teeth.

"What would you ladies like?" the bartender asked.

"Two dirty martinis with bleu cheese olives," Carrie responded.

Glancing over at her, I noticed the Cheshire cat grin on her face. "What are you smiling about?"

"Just taking in the scene. I mean, have you ever seen a room full of this many good-looking men? It's like a smorgasbord of fine and sexy. Maybe I should do a little game of eenie-meenie-miney-mo."

I looked around and couldn't help but agree. Including the man who'd caught my attention when I walked in, amazingly handsome men surrounded us, all of them oozing sensual temptation. "Damn, girl. How'd you even know we could get in here? This looks like an exclusive club. Not that I'm complaining."

"Remember that banquet I went to a few weeks ago? The one you refused to attend with me?"

I gave her a side-eye. "Carrie, I can't always be your plus-one." That was one night my parents honestly couldn't watch Malachi, and I wasn't too pressed about it. I hadn't really wanted to go to a banquet and eat rubber chicken.

"Yes, you can, but that's not the point. What I was saying is that I overheard some people talking about this place. How exclusive it is to live here, that they cater to wealthy, single bachelors, and that women come here to the bar to hang out, snag a rich boyfriend, and for the occasional fun experience."

Looking around at the women laughing and talking to the men, I couldn't help but read their body language and the openly flirtatious glances. Oooohhh... Oh! My head swiveled back to the man who'd caught my attention, only to find him staring at me from across the room. Oh. Damn.

Tapping Carrie's arm, I leaned over to her. "So, you mean none of these women live here?"

"Nope," she said, shaking her head.

"Do the men know why the women are here? You know, to snag a rich boyfriend or have a night of fun?"

"Yup," Carrie smiled over at me.

The usual twinkle in her eyes was present, and I knew I'd been had. "You did this on purpose." This girl was lucky that she was such a good friend because I would have left her ass right here.

Turning to me, she nodded. "I sure did. Listen. Even if you do nothing tonight or you don't meet anyone you want to continue talking to, I want you to look around."

I did. "Why?"

"Do you see all the men looking at you?"

"Yes," especially the blond sitting in the chair. "I do. So what?"

"Honey, you've been holed up in your house for too long watching over my godson. I know you, Anya, and I have some hard truths for you. You think the world has left you behind because you got pregnant and had a child. Now, you know I love my godson as if I birthed him my damn self, but sweetheart, just because you had a child doesn't mean your life is over."

I know she meant well. I did. But it was always difficult when I met someone and thought we clicked on so many levels, only to see the light in their eyes dim when I shared with them that I was a single mother raising a small son. That kind of rejection, not only of me but of my son, was not something I wanted to repeat.

"I know it's not," I finally responded. "But I need to focus on teaching Malachi his numbers and ABCs so he can be ready for preschool. The men I've met aren't interested in dating a single mother. That's too much baggage for them." It hurt to say the words because my son was a blessing to my life, but I also knew my words were the truth.

"Then that's why this place is so perfect."

"Why?" I knew that tone, and I was positive I would not like the response.

"Just look around us. The world is your oyster. You can choose to do whatever you want or don't want. If talking is all you need tonight, then talk. But maybe… just maybe… you might find someone you're interested in knowing a little better. The men here have been vetted, and by that, I mean they've investigated every aspect of their life before allowing them into the Tower. It's time for us to turn the tables on them."

My mouth fell open as I listened to Carrie speak. Could I be brave enough to let go and let things happen? It's not that I was someone who shied away from having fun, but there always seemed to be something else more important than playing the dating game.

Could I really do this? Was I ready to do this?

"Let's find a table and sit down. I don't want to be standing on five-inch heels all night." Turning to the bartender, I got his attention. "Can we pay for these now? We want to find a table and sit down."

He gave me a slight tilt of his lips. I couldn't help but think this place also must have an attractiveness test. How is it that every single man in this room was panty-dropping sexy? "Your tab has been taken care of for the night. Order whatever you'd like."

Carrie let out a squeal of delight next to me. I gave her a look meant to express that she needed to settle her ass down.

"Do you know who paid our tab? Since we came together and don't know anyone here, I'd like to know who we should thank for their courtesy." And hopefully, the man wasn't expecting anything in return.

"Yes. He's the man sitting in the chair over near the fireplace. Blond hair. Black suit. Green shirt." The bartender lifted his head and nodded at someone behind us. Turning my head, I noticed the guy who'd caught my eye when we walked in, standing up from his chair.

Oh, fuck!

"Um, thank you." I turned to Carrie and caught her gaze. "We need to go thank him for taking care of our drinks tonight."

She had a smile on her face, but her eyes widened as another man stood up across from the blond. This man had dark hair, wore jeans, and a collared shirt with a pullover on top. What the fuck? Did they pull these fuckers off the pages of a magazine?

"Yes," Carrie said breathlessly. "Let's definitely go thank them."

Grabbing our drinks, we began walking over to the two men. The closer we got to them, the more nervous I became. He never took his eyes off me and the butterflies took flight in my stomach. Why did it feel like this moment would change my life forever? I only hoped it would be for the best.

Three
Hunter

Watching the woman in the black dress walk in my direction, I had to hold back the urge to rush over, grab her up, and take her upstairs to my apartment. From the moment I saw her across the room, I knew she was the one for me.

Patience wasn't one of my virtues, especially when it came to something, or someone, I wanted. But as I tracked her progress in my direction, something about the look in her eyes gave me pause. As she and her friend came closer to Bryce and me, I shifted.

Stretching my shoulders, I rolled my neck to relieve some of the stress. Her eyes widened, and I saw her steps stutter. Hmmmm, that was interesting. I couldn't help but smile at her reaction. They were taking too long to get over to us, so I stepped forward.

"Hello, ladies," I greeted as I walked up to her. She had to be no more than five-seven. Maybe five-eight. Those damn heels were distorting her height. Didn't matter to me, because even in those heels, she was still at least half a foot shorter than me. "Hunter Malone."

I watched as she glanced at her friend, who gave her a smile and a slight nod. "Anya Newton."

Next to me, I heard Bryce introduce himself to her friend. Not that I cared if he did or not. My entire purpose was to get her… Anya, over to me. "Would you like to sit down?"

Her friend answered for them. "Yes. Thank you."

Her friend sat in the chair next to Bryce. After a moment of hesitation, Anya sat down next to me.

She captured my attention from the jump. There was no way I could take my gaze from Anya. From her jerky motions, I could tell she was skittish. Maybe even a bit nervous. I could even see a hint of burgundy bloom on her brown cheeks. I wanted to smile at her reaction to me, but didn't want to scare her off. Glancing down, I couldn't help but appreciate her toned brown legs. She wore red toenail paint, which I could see through her peep-toe shoes, which seemed extremely sexy to me. One hand cradled the martini glass as she took a sip, a bit of the liquid resting on her lips. She stuck her tongue out to wipe at the wetness and I could have sworn I fucking moaned.

Maybe this was a bad idea. I'm not sure how the hell I was supposed to survive sitting here with her when her every movement took me down a rabbit hole of picturing her lying beneath me on my bed as she screamed my name.

"So, what brought you beautiful ladies to our humble dwelling?" Bryce asked the blonde, Ashley... Carrie... whatever.

As the woman answered the question, I tuned her out and focused on the beautiful goddess next to me. "Thank you for accepting my offer." Staring into her face, I noticed she looked a little skittish, avoiding my gaze. As I continued to wait for her to answer, I never took my eyes off her face. "Cat got your tongue?"

Her lips tilted in a smile. "You're welcome. Then again, did I really have a choice?" Her brown eyes bored into mine as she challenged me.

I wanted to blurt out things I'd never said before. Hell, at this point, if she kept her gaze on me this way, I'd promise her the fucking world. "Beautiful Anya. You always have a choice." And she did. But that didn't mean I wouldn't do everything in my power to make sure her choice always landed on me.

She smiled, dipping her head shyly before returning her gaze to mine. "Um, we just met. Isn't it too early for endearments and sweet nicknames?"

"No," I responded. "It's never too early to speak the truth. You are beautiful. I'm just sharing how I see you."

She giggled, turning her face away for a bit as if looking around the space. Her eyes landed on her friend, who was in an intensely private conversation with Bryce. Turning back to me, she lifted her glass and took another sip of her drink. "Why did you pay for our drinks?"

"Because I wanted to meet you." Might as well go with the truth. I was never one for lies, and usually, that was how people got caught up.

"Okay, well, you've met me. Now what?" Shifting her body, she turned toward me.

"Now, we spend some time talking and getting to know each other." I leaned toward her, getting closer. My nostrils flared as the scent of her reached me. "I noticed you as soon as you walked inside."

Her eyes traveled over my entire face, and I could see the small smile come over her lips. "There are a lot of beautiful women here tonight."

Glancing around, I took in all the ladies lounging around before returning my gaze to Anya. "Yes, there are. Even your friend is incredibly beautiful." The smile on her face faltered for a slight second. "But you are the only one who captured my attention. I don't buy drinks for women I don't know."

Lifting her glass, she tilted it up, swallowing down the last of her drink. "You bought me a drink. Along with Carrie, of course."

Shaking my head, I glanced at Bryce. "He'll pay me back for that later. Technically, it will only be your drinks I pay for."

"Why?"

"Because I want you in my bed tonight." The look in her eyes made me laugh, which is not something I do very often. "Does that surprise you?"

"I'm not sure. You're very sure of yourself. What if I didn't want to be in your bed?"

I leaned back before resting my ankle on my bent knee. "Sweetheart, you already made that decision when you were watching me at the bar. You don't have to hide what you want.

I'm not one for hiding behind societal norms. You can admit you want me just as much as I want you."

"You're something else," she said, her eyes not leaving my face. "I should be offended."

I shrugged. "You say that, but the question is, are you?"

After a moment's pause, she shook her head. "No. We literally met ten minutes ago, and you already invited me to sleep with you. Who does that?"

"Because I know what I want. Why wait? The result will be the same."

Anya sat next to me silent with her drink half-lifted to her lips. She had every right to question my words. Although technically, she was correct; we hadn't known each other long. I was planning to change that. "As soon as my eyes landed on you, I knew I wanted to spend time with you. Preferably naked, but if all I can get is drinks and great conversation, I'll take that as well."

Her hands started fidgeting and her eyes darted around the table.

"Would you like another drink?" I asked, a bit of teasing in my voice.

"Yes," she breathed out, staring at me.

Raising my hand, I called over the waiter, placing an order for another dirty martini with bleu cheese olives and my favorite fifteen-year-old scotch. "Now, where were we?" She smiled at me and I could feel myself thickening under my slacks.

"Well, we were going to get to know each other as we enjoyed a drink," she responded.

Leaning forward, I got closer to her face. My eyes dropped down to her lips. "Is that all?"

She sighed, but this time there was a smile to go along with it. "It's a start."

I nodded in agreement. After all, the night was young. There was plenty of time, and

I was happy to play the long game. "So, Anya Newton. Tell me something about you."

"No, I don't think I want to start," she said, shaking her head. "How about we start with you? I think your life will be a lot more interesting than mine. Have you lived here long?"

Just then, the waiter brought our drinks back and sat them down in front of us. Lifting my glass, I held it up in front of me. "A toast?" As she lifted her glass, I could feel something inside me shift. I didn't know what was happening, but I knew this was the start of something different for me. "How about let's toast to us getting to know each other better?"

She tapped her glass against mine. "Yes, I'm looking forward to it."

We both took a sip before setting our drinks down. "Now, to answer your question, I've lived here for a couple of years."

"According to Carrie, it's really hard to get a spot."

"It is," I acknowledged. "Once you're here, you rarely leave. Not unless you get married or die."

"Wait a minute. You mean to tell me that all the men who live here are single and ready to mingle?" Anya then laughed at her own joke.

Corny, yes, but I enjoyed seeing the smile on her face. "Yes, I guess you could call it that."

"What about you, Anya? Why are you here tonight?" I wanted to know if there was more to the woman sitting across from me.

"I needed a night out. Carrie heard of this place and thought it would be fun."

"This isn't your normal scene when you go out?" Thank fuck, because I would hate to think I'd connected so strongly with someone just looking to hook up with someone rich.

She shook her head, "Oh no. I'm usually in my house watching a movie, recovering from

a long day at work, and hanging with Ma—."
Clearing her throat, she took another sip of her
martini.

"Hanging with who?" I couldn't help but
prod.

"Just hanging out, usually with my
friends. I have some family in the area."

While I didn't think that was the whole
truth, I wasn't going to call her out on it. "If
you're here tonight, I take it you're not seeing
anyone?"

She laughed. "I'm definitely not seeing
anyone."

"Good." That meant she was mine for the
taking.

"Good?"

"Yeah, that's good. I'd hate to have you
break some other man's heart when I take you
away from him." And honestly, I would do it in
a heartbeat because Anya was too beautiful to
let go.

"How do you know I could be taken by you or anyone else?"

I stayed silent for a minute, watching her as she tried to hold my gaze. "Beautiful, there's no doubt I could take you from any man in your life. I just need you to open the door."

"You just met me."

Nodding, I responded. "Yes, but we're both adults. We know what we want. We know how to keep things simple. I want you. I've made that clear. So, are you hungry?" It took a minute for my words to register.

"What? Wait, what? Am I hungry?"

Yeah, sweetheart, I'm gonna keep you guessing. "Yes, they have some good food here. If you're hungry, we should eat. I have a feeling it's going to be a long night." Watching her, I knew this was going to be the start of something good. Not that I was looking for anything long-term, but having a beautiful woman in my arms was always welcome.

Glancing at her up and down once more, I licked my lips as I couldn't help thinking about how sweet she'd taste.

A soft smile came over her lips. "How long of a night are you planning for us?"

"Oh, sweetheart, you have no idea." I planned to feast on her all night if she allowed me.

"Just come with me to grab some food. Promise you'll enjoy yourself." And I meant that with every fiber of my being.

Four
Anya

If you asked me later how I ended up in Hunter's apartment, I wouldn't be able to tell you. Or maybe I did, and I just didn't want to admit it. Oh, hell. Fine, you pulled it out of me. The truth?

The man is fine as hell. He made me laugh, and I couldn't help but wonder if he was big all over. If the old wives' tale of big hands and big feet were true, then he was definitely who I'd been looking for tonight.

It had been too long for me—years, in fact. I'd been busy raising my son and living my life. I wasn't worried about finding a man. That wasn't a priority for me. But tonight, meeting Hunter had flipped a switch in me. His voice was smooth and deep and smoky. Confidence oozed from every pore of his being. It was as if he knew all the women in the room wanted to be with him, while the men wanted to be him. The man knew who he was and what he wanted. And at least for tonight, he swore up and down he wanted me.

Who was I to question why he'd lost his mind?

What I needed to do was focus on why my panties were gone and my legs wrapped around his waist as he held me up against his hard length. My clit tingled, pulsing with each press of his hard length against my core.

I mean, the drinks were great. Dinner was excellent. A few hours into the evening, Carrie left with Bryce after she promised to text me. She and I both knew the drill. Text our location and take a non-flash picture of our surroundings. It was just a safety precaution. We hadn't used it often, but tonight was going to be the exception.

He pressed my back against the closed door. Our lips fused together, each of us fighting for dominance. His kisses felt so good, melting me from the inside out. I could feel my body responding, preparing for what was about to happen next. My channel clenched in need, want, and desire. If you asked me tomorrow how I got myself in this situation, my answer would be simple.

I wanted this. I needed this.

His words and the look in his eyes promised me a night to remember, and I was taking the gift he offered.

Maybe the better answer would be I needed Hunter because I'd become the captured prey.

"Stop thinking so much," Hunter whispered against my neck.

"Make me," I challenged. I have no idea where this sassy person came from, but I liked her style. I may keep her around a bit more.

His lips tilted in a smile. The look on his face should have worried me. It didn't. I wanted more. Leaning forward, I captured his lips with mine, deepening the kiss. His arms tightened around my ass, holding me close to him as he turned us toward the hallway. Breaking away from our kiss, I leaned back and looked at him a bit closer. He stared at me right back.

"You're so damn beautiful, Anya," he whispered into the darkness of the room.

I wanted to challenge his statement, but what good would that do? The man was holding me in his arms as he walked us to his bedroom. I'm positive he wasn't planning on reading me a bedtime story. We were about to do some serious boom-chicka-now-now, so who the hell was I to tell him how to feel about me.

Maybe he had bad eyes or something and forget his glasses earlier.

Oh well, I knew there had to be something wrong with him because he was just too damn perfect. It didn't matter at this point.

"Thank you. You're not so bad yourself." What else was there to say? Yup, not a damn thing.

As he walked into his bedroom, I didn't have a chance to look around because he threw me down on the bed, my body bouncing slightly as I settled into the softness of the bed comforter.

My brain and body went into overdrive. Who the hell was this man to just handle me as if I were a rag doll? Damn, that shit was sexy as hell.

He walked over to the bed, his hand trailing up my almost bare leg. A shiver of excitement went through my body as his touch ignited something inside me. Looking up at him, his blue eyes captured mine. I felt enthralled. I felt as if I were floating. My legs shifted and moved as I tried to quiet the ache growing inside me. Everywhere he touched, I felt electricity. Tightening my lips, I held back the moan fighting its way out.

"Why are you holding back from me?" His voice sounded rough. If I didn't know better, I would think the words were being forced from his throat. His need for me was reflected on his face.

Did he not realize what he was doing to me? Had he practiced this in the mirror? Yeah, he absolutely had to because there was no way this was natural.

"Anya. Open up for me."

Why was I shaking in anticipation? Oh, I know why. If the imprint inside his pants was any indication, he was about to blow my back out. That's what I'd wanted earlier, right?

My panties were soaked, and I know he could see my nipples hardening as he spoke. On the one hand, I was embarrassed that he could so easily tell just how much I wanted him. Then again, I was a grown-ass woman determined to have fun tonight. Maybe I would be more worried if I were here with him and my panties were dry as toast. Wouldn't that be some shit? So, I did what he asked and widened my legs to see precisely what he was doing to me.

His eyes widened. Nostrils flared. Lips tilted up in a smirk. "Yes, that's what I thought." Leaning down, he captured my lips in a kiss. Our tongues dueled, my body arched up toward him, trying to get as close as I could. There were too many barriers between us. I wanted to feel our skin touching. It was like I'd been waiting for this for so long. This moment. With Hunter.

He lifted slightly, smiling down at me. "I want you naked. You can do it yourself, or I can."

Shit, I didn't need to be told twice. As I moved and began removing my shoes, he stepped back, chuckling. I glanced at him as I stripped. "I know what I want, so why pretend otherwise," I said with a soft laugh.

He pulled his shirt off, baring his chest to my gaze. If the ancient gods truly existed, then Hunter had to be a descendent of Zeus. There was a smattering of hair covering his skin, and I wanted to reach out and run my fingers through it. He'd unbuttoned his pants, the black boxers underneath peeking out over the loosened clasp. "I'm glad we're no longer pretending," he said with a smile.

I removed my bra. My panties were the only thing remaining. Hunter quickly shucked his pants and underwear, showing his entire body to my gaze. Now it was my turn to stare and if I wasn't mistaken, that low whimper I heard was coming from me. My mouth watered at the sight in front of me. His member was thickening under my eyes and I felt my channel becoming slick with desire.

"Like what you see?" Hunter asked, taking a step closer to me.

Licking my lips, I responded. "Yes. Very much."

"Good. I'm happy to hear that." Hunter cradled my face in his hands, placing soft kisses on my lips, jaw, and shoulders. "I'm so very pleased you showed up tonight."

Using his body, he pushed me back onto the bed. Shifting, he positioned himself over me, resting between my legs. "I'm going to make you a very happy woman tonight."

"Then you'd better get busy."

***

My body ached in places it shouldn't. My internal alarm clock must have kicked in because when my eyes opened, the sun was just making its way over the horizon. A low-grade headache was making its way through my skull, but it wasn't anything I couldn't handle. Stretching my legs, I felt some discomfort in my lower region and couldn't help the smile that came over my face. Hunter most definitely came through last night.

Of course, when I agreed to go out with Carrie, I hadn't been expecting to meet someone and sleep with him. Not that I hadn't had my fun in my early years, but I was a responsible woman, a mother, and focused on just trying to make it each day. Sleeping with uber-rich men in their multi-million-dollar apartment in a crazy, exclusive building wasn't my usual approach. If I think about it, and sometimes I try not to, my last time having this type of fun had been before my son was born. Sad, yes. But those are the facts.

Looking over my shoulder at the man lying in bed with me, I couldn't help the giggle that escaped. This was fun. Hunter had been fantastic. Mind-blowing, if I wanted to be honest. But now the fun was over. It was time for me to head home and get back to reality again. The memories of last night, and early this morning, would carry me for a long time. The way he worshipped every inch of my body, whispering soft words in my ear as he brought me to the edge repeatedly. Just thinking about it again made my body tingle with need.

"No, Anya. Get your ass up and get home," I whispered to myself. I needed to remember what this was. A one-time trip to the wild side. Rising slowly from the bed, I looked back to make sure Hunter was still sleeping. He was.

Mentally lecturing myself to get out now before he woke up, I tamped down the regret bubbling to the surface. One thing I knew was that I'd never forget this experience. Even though I was running away from the one man who'd made me feel sexy and desirable for the first time in over three years, I would keep the visions of what we did close to my heart, only pulling out the memories when by myself at night in the comfort of my own bed.

But for me, being a mom was my entire focus. My little guy was the only person I needed in my life. Did it get lonely? Yes. Did I want to be held at night? Absolutely. But that wasn't my life right now and I sure as hell would not nominate millionaire business owner Hunter Malone for the job.

It didn't matter that he made me feel seen as a woman for the first time in years. I shouldn't care that he spent all our time together focused on my pleasure. My moans.

My whimpers. It would be ridiculous of me to put too much into a one-night stand.

Finally gathering all my stuff, I hastily dressed. Pulling my hair back, I twisted it into a quick bun that stopped me from looking as if I'd just come from an all-night sexcapade. Yay, score one for mom's always being prepared. I took one more look around the room and knew it was time to go. Did I want to climb right back into that bed and beg him for more? Damn skippy, I did. But I had put the wild and free Anya back inside her comfortable, safe box.

Using an app on my phone, I scheduled a car to pick me up out front. For a moment, I wondered how many times this happened to him? How many women did he bring up to his apartment for the night, did things to their bodies that made them addicted to his touch, only for them to leave the following day craving more, but too afraid to take that step and tell him?

It wasn't that I was afraid to ask for what I wanted. No. Not at all. I needed to leave because I could feel myself being pulled back to him. Back to the feeling he gave me. That's how I knew it was time for me to go. Closing the door behind me, I suddenly realized my mistake. Women weren't supposed to be in the hallways alone. There were strict rules about it. Hunter even mentioned it a time or two last night.

Decision time.

Do I take the risk and walk out of here on my own, or do I eat some humble pie and knock on the door to wake up Hunter so he can escort me out?

Just as I was about to ring the doorbell to Hunter's apartment, a voice stopped me. "Are you trying to sneak back in or want to sneak out?"

I turned around to look at the man and could do nothing but stare up at him in awe. What was it about living here? Did every man who owned a place here look like sex personified?

"Um. Well, technically, I wasn't doing anything just yet. Plus, sneaking is such a dirty word. Let's just say it's time for me to get back to reality."

The dark-haired man across from me, dressed for the gym, just smiled in my direction before raising one eyebrow in question. "Reality, huh?" He glanced up at the door and shook his head. "Hunter's not gonna be happy that you left without telling him."

"How do you know he doesn't already know? I'm an independent woman," I snarked. He could call my bluff if he wanted to. Something must have stopped him, because he only dipped his head down the hallway. "Hunter's gonna be pissed, but I have no choice. Come on. I'll escort you downstairs. If you're caught in our hallways on your own, that would be a huge problem."

Now I was having second thoughts. I mean, who was this man? He came out of nowhere, and now suddenly, he was going to escort me safely down to the lobby. I quickly snapped a picture.

He laughed. "Really? You know what? Go ahead and snap your picture. My name is Phil. I live on this floor. My apartment is right here, next to Hunter's."

"A woman can never be too safe," I say, sending his photo to Carrie with a note asking her where the hell she was.

Looking over at Hunter's door, he shook his head. "No, a woman can never be too safe. Let's get you downstairs."

Five
Hunter

It's been three days since my night with Anya. I'm still pissed about Anya leaving in the morning without telling me, by the way. How the hell did I sleep through her leaving my bed and the door closing behind her? Then again, I know exactly why. She put it on me so good; I was out like a light. Probably for the first time in years.

As I stood here stewing in frustration that she'd left without my knowledge, I could admit to myself that the entire night with Anya was burned into my memory. No matter how much I tried to put her out of my mind, and nothing I did helped me forget the look on her face as she came undone as I was inside her body. The feel of her soft skin was seared into my soul. Before I realized it, I was rubbing my hands together just thinking about touching her again.

It was like I couldn't get enough of her, and it had only been one night. But that one night was something I wanted to have on repeat. Every time I thought we were done, that I was sated, I needed her again. Just one more time. If I had to count how many times I had sunk inside her body, losing myself in the feeling of having her underneath me or on top of me, I wouldn't be able to tell you.

When I woke up that morning and realized she'd left without a word, a note, or anything, I was pissed. To be honest, I'm not the type of man to bring women up to my apartment. And when I do, I always make sure they know the deal. One night only. No expectations beyond that. More times than not, I'm the one calling up a car service for them in the morning as I feed them breakfast.

Yes, of course, I feed them. I'm a gentleman, not a neanderthal.

I'm not the type of man to do entanglements. As beautiful as they are, women always came with something that made them a little too much. Ex-boyfriends, expensive habits, greedy relatives. Didn't matter what the issue was; there was always something. Why would Anya be any different? Her leaving without saying anything was the best possible solution. At least that's what I tried to convince myself when I woke up Saturday.

I paced my bedroom conjuring up her face, smile, body, and scent. Forgetting about her was the best option for me. My business was my focus. That's all I needed right now. That lasted for all of one hour.

Then I went back to being pissed. It wasn't me who kicked her out. She'd left on her own. Snuck out like a thief in the damn night. Hell, the least she could have done was leave a note. Her number. Something. She didn't even give me a chance to tell her if I wanted more. She just assumed. Did she think so low of herself? Or did she think that way about me?

By all definitions, I was living the high life. The large window behind my desk had a perfect view of the Charles River. Looking out at the view, I knew I should be proud of everything I'd accomplished. I wasn't going to lie, getting to this point had taken years of hard work. It took me years to make something of myself and build a business that I was proud of. My business was growing, my life was going exactly the way I expected, and if I had a need,

I could have almost any woman I wanted with the snap of my fingers.

Then why did I still want Anya so much?

Sighing, I closed my eyes. My mind immediately began to replay our time together. She was on top of me, my hands cradling her hips as I thrust inside her. Her hands grabbed my chest, her moans of pleasure like music to my ears. Above me, she looked like an angel. Too bad I was the wicked devil whispering in her ear to do naughty things with me all night long. I wasn't sure why this woman affected me the way she did. All I knew was that she did.

Opening my eyes, I took a deep breath. I needed to stop thinking about her. She left.

To me, that meant she also felt our time together was limited. Anya knew the game and played it well. I was the only one sitting here moping over something I couldn't control. Women didn't get to me. I never let myself get caught up in how I felt about a woman. This was sure as fuck not going to be the first time it happened.

A knock on my door announced my secretary stepping inside. "Hunter. Your two o'clock meeting has arrived. They're waiting for you in the conference room."

Turning and nodding, I walked toward my desk. "Thanks, Natalie. I'll be there in five minutes."

"Yes, sir," she said with a smile as she closed the door.

Natalie's title may be secretary, but she ran my company with an iron fist. She kept me on schedule, didn't allow others to have access to me without approval, and when I said I wanted something done, she made sure it happened.

It didn't matter if others were in charge of completing the project. Natalie was a godsend, and no matter how many times I told her not to call me Sir, she did it anyway. I knew it was only because she liked to bust my balls. But Natalie was the only one given that leeway. Unlike everyone else who tried it, I took what she dished out because that woman was worth her weight in gold. Walking from my office five minutes later, I nodded to Natalie as she sat behind her desk.

"You're late. You said five minutes."

"They can wait," I called back. Yes, I respected the time of anyone who came to see me and got on my calendar. That didn't mean I lived my life based on someone else's schedule. I'd be there when I arrived, and they'd deal with it or get the fuck out of my offices.

I was committed to putting Anya out of my mind and focusing on my business. Today was important to me. If things went well, it would catapult my company into the next stratosphere. I didn't have time to focus on a woman, no matter how beautiful, sexy, or intelligent she was.

When I walked into this room to meet with the investors, they'd expect the shark to show up. Not a man too focused on getting between a woman's thighs that he couldn't focus on the business at hand. The memory of Anya would have to be put in a box. Tucked away in the recesses of my brain. I didn't have time to think about a woman who couldn't be bothered with leaving a fucking note.

And there I went, getting pissed off all over again. This shit was all upside down. Women didn't just get up and walk out on me. There was a pattern to these things. I treat them well for the night, then we wake up and have a short repeat to make sure they have a memory to keep them warm at night. Next, I always make them breakfast in the morning. Can't have them out in the world on an empty stomach, right? A car was always waiting for them once they filled their stomachs. No matter how many times someone tried to have another go at me, I resisted. That wasn't how I played the game. But Anya... yeah, I would have invited her to stay for a while longer. There were so many other things I wanted to do with her.

Fuck, this shit was messing with my head.

I saw my Chief Operating Officer step out of the room. No surprise there. I'm sure everyone was wondering where I was. "Hey, Dan. Everyone ready?"

"They are. I came out to find you. You good?"

Nodding, I stepped to the door. "Let's close this deal," I said before stepping inside. All thoughts of Anya had to be forced from my mind. It was time to focus on my next favorite thing. Making money.

***

Okay, fine. My resolve to forget about her lasted until the meeting was complete and made it back to my office.

I stayed focused for the marathon session of over three hours, just enough time to get things where I wanted them to be for this deal. The investors needed some additional convincing, which was fine by me. Since we were talking to them about their company investing over twenty-five million with us, the time was needed. If they wanted a couple more product demonstrations and detailed answers on the company financials, I was willing to give them what they needed. Within reason. Looking back on the meeting, I knew this deal would go through.

No more than thirty minutes after all the hand shaking had finished, and they'd left the building, my mind turned right back to the person I'd been thinking about for the last three days.

Anya Newton.

I needed to talk to her.

The piece of paper in my hand that held many of the answers I wanted. Anya's telephone number, address, and where she worked. If I wanted to end the torture, all I had to do was pick up my phone and call her. But if I did that, what do I want to happen? I've sworn off relationships, but for Anya, I might consider it.

Then again, did I really want the drama and stress of a woman in my life? I smiled. Maybe things would be different with her.

Who the hell was I trying to convince? Myself?

I didn't need to convince myself of anything. I knew what I wanted. Who I wanted. Anya may think we're done, but we're far from over. Looking over at the clock, I noticed it was after eight. Grabbing up my keys, I made my way out of the office. The piece of paper still burned a hole in my pocket.

When I reached out to my connection, Conall O'Shea, I wasn't sure if I was doing the right thing. I've known him for quite some time, and he's always done right by me, just as I've done right by him. Conall was someone good to have on your side, especially when you need something a little suspect. When I called him and asked for his help, he made sure the price of his cooperation was a future dinner with him and his wife, Tatiana. I sometimes wondered if she knew the extent of Conall's business dealings, but then again, it wasn't my concern.

Once in my car and on the road, my fingers began itching to talk to Anya. I hated this feeling of indecisiveness. It wasn't like me. When I wanted something, I went after it. I was relentless. Pulling over to the side of the road, I pulled out the piece of paper with the telephone number I'd been starting at all day. Even though I probably had it memorized, I didn't want to make a mistake.

Fuck this. I didn't beg, and I sure as hell didn't chase.

But that didn't stop me from thinking about her. I needed to either get over this fascination I had with Anya, or I needed to do what the fuck I'd been thinking about all day. Calling her. Letting her know I wanted to see her again. Claiming her body again. Damn, just thinking about her had me hardening in my pants.

Sitting here on the side of the road wasn't doing me any good. I wasn't calling her tonight. Pulling back onto the road, I continued to my apartment. If I were going to do this, I needed a plan. Running her off or scaring her wasn't what I wanted. I'm sure calling her out of the blue wouldn't be the best way to get things started off right.

Then it hit me. Activating the voice call function in the car, I called up Bryce.

"Hey, Hunter. What's up, man?"

"Are you still in touch with Carrie from the other night?" This was my connection to get to Anya. This wasn't creepy at all, right?

He was silent for a moment, but then he spoke. "Yeah. I'm probably gonna see her again. Why?"

"I think it's time to arrange a double-date."

Did I really just say that? What the fuck? Was I in high school again? Didn't matter. I'd do whatever it takes, play whatever role I needed to play, just to see Anya again.

Six
Anya

Regret coursed through me from the moment I walked out of the Tower. Now, six days later, I'm questioning why I was such an idiot. No one cares that I slept with one of the most eligible bachelors in Boston. The only people who knew were Carrie, Hunter's friend Bryce, and that guy Phil who walked me out of the building that next day.

I still don't know why I ran from his apartment that morning. Sure, I can tell myself it was because I wanted to take back control and not become one of "those" women. I felt it was important that I walk out on him before he told me to leave. Embarrassment wasn't something I wanted to go through, and after a night like we had, being shown the door was the last thing I wanted.

So, I left.

Then I immediately wished I hadn't.

"Mommy? I'm hungry. Chicken nuggets?"

Glancing down at Malachi, my heart squeezed with love for my child. He was only three years old, but he made my life worth living. When I first discovered I was pregnant by my ex-boyfriend, I thought my life was over. Traveling the globe. Going back to school. Partying on all seven continents. All the plans I'd made for myself went up in smoke. Or so I'd believed.

My life goals may have changed, but that doesn't mean my life was over. It just meant I had to re-evaluate my plans and take a different approach. Once Malachi turned five, we were hopping on the first plane out of here. Of course, we'd return after our adventures were complete. I still had to work, and those trips had to be funded somehow.

"You're going to turn into a nugget," I laughed in return.

"I'm not a nugget. You're a nugget, Momma," he said with a huge smile. "Nuggets, please."

Even though his words weren't clear, I could still understand him. Sometimes he was the sweetest little boy ever. Other times, he was… precocious and energetic. Either way, he was all mine, and I loved every minute of the life I'd created with my little prince.

"Okay, sweetheart. You can have chicken nuggets tonight. Do momma a favor and pick up your toys for me. Okay?"

He nodded before running off towards the front room. I knew that would keep him busy for the next ten minutes. Not a long time, but enough to get a breather. When Carrie's ring tone sounded in the room, I swiped the screen.

"Hey, lady. What's up?"

"Heeeeyyyy, Anya."

Oh damn, I knew that tone. Carrie was setting me up for something, and I honestly wanted nothing to do with it. The last time she convinced me to step out of my comfort zone, it turned into... well, the best night of my life, other than the day Malachi was born. Then again, almost one week later, and here I was. Still thinking about that mistake and considering whether I want to risk it all again for a small taste.

"Carrie. I know that tone in your voice. You want something, and I'm not giving it to you."

She laughed. "You don't even know what I'm going to say."

I shook my head, even though she couldn't see me. "Nope. I'm not falling for it again. Sorry, hon, but I'm not going out tonight. I don't have a sitter, I have to work tomorrow, and I'm still not fully recovered from the last time you drug me outside."

A deep sigh came across the phone. "Oh, no. Don't you even try to take that tone with me. I know you had an amazing time last Friday. Want to know how I know this?"

Even though she couldn't see me, I rolled my eyes at her question. "No, I don't. Because it's going to be some convoluted explanation about synergy and fate or some other such mess."

"Very funny," Carrie responded. "Don't worry, I'm going to tell you anyway."

Pulling out the ingredients for dinner, I laughed. "As I knew you would. So, tell me, oh wise one. How do you know I had an amazing time?"

Carrie cleared her throat. "Because you're scared to talk about him. From the moment you left his place the next morning, you've been tight-lipped about what happened between the two of you."

I knew she'd figure it out. She's known me too damn long. "Maybe I don't want to tell you all the details of my night, Carrie. Some things should stay private." As soon as I said the words, I knew she was going to jump on them.

"Oh! Is that what we're doing now? Girl, nothing has been private between us since we met each other in college our sophomore year. I know all your secrets, just like you know mine. I shared with you everything that happened with Bryce, but when I asked you about your tall drink of milk, you clammed up on me. That's not like you. Usually, with me, you're an open book. So, try that crap with someone else.

You're holding back for a reason. I want to know why."

Okay, fine. Maybe she was right. "Having you as a best friend is very annoying," I quipped, removing some vegetables from the fridge. Even though I caved on the chicken nuggets request, that didn't mean I couldn't add in something to make me feel better as a mother. Green beans were now on the menu, and little man would have to deal with it.

"No, having me as a best friend is your life's second greatest gift. The first, of course, is that you're a mom to my little nugget. By the way, where is he?"

"I'm here, auntie Carrie," Malachi called out as he raced around the room.

"Hey, Punkin' Pie," Carrie called out to him.

Smiling at their antics, you'd think I didn't exist in the room when these two were around each other. "Carrie, I know you called me for a reason, and I'm still not sure I want to hear it."

She cleared her throat. "Well, since you asked so nicely. What are you doing tomorrow night?"

I rolled my eyes because the last time she asked me this question, I met Hunter. I'm not sure if I wanted to go through anything like that again. If we went out, I'd probably compare every man who dared approached me to him. It would no doubt turn into a miserable and unhappy night.

Not that I want to meet anyone new, but I also didn't want to have Hunter on my mind the entire time. After our night together, I knew few men could compare to him, so why even try?

"I'm not doing anything tomorrow night, which you already know." Not that I didn't want to go out, but I had to protect my heart and my sanity. "Carrie, I can't do it. I don't want to go out and meet another guy. Last week was enough for me. Honestly, the memories will last me a very long time." Just thinking about the things that man did to my body had me all hot and bothered.

"Damn. He put it on you like that?"

I sighed loudly in response. *Yes. Yes, he sure as hell did.* "Girl, you don't even know the half of it."

Her laugh came through the phone. "Well, then you definitely want to line up a babysitter for tomorrow night. You know I've been talking to Bryce since we met them last week, right?"

Nodding to myself, I continued preparing dinner for Malachi and me. "Good for you." Yes, I was happy for my friend, but it also disappointed me that Hunter hadn't made more effort to contact me.

"No, honey. Good for us. Bryce wants to see me tomorrow night. He said you should also come because Hunter wants to see you."

"How does he know that?" I questioned, but didn't wait to hear the answer. "Listen, I love you, but I'm not trying to tag along like the desperate friend who's begging for more. If he wanted to see me, then he could have reached out to me. Called. Texted. Something."

There was a moment of silence. "Oh, so you *did* give him your number?"

Well, fuck, she had me there. No, I didn't give him anything other than my name. Anyway, that's beside the damn point. He was a rich and successful man. I'm positive he has resources and could find whatever information he needed. That he hadn't used all his super-rich man powers to find me made my stomach clench. I feared our night together meant more to me than him, and I wasn't trying to go through the pain of rejection. Not now. Not never.

"I didn't hear your answer, Anya," Carrie pressed. "Did you give him your number for him to call you?"

"No, I didn't," I finally admitted.

"And there we go. Listen, girl, I'm not doing this with you. Stop hiding and get out there and live your life. Did you not tell me that you were the one who snuck out of his apartment like you were trying to get out of paying rent?"

"It was for the best," I mumbled. If I kept telling myself that, maybe I'd start to believe it.

Carrie ignored me. "Maybe he didn't think you wanted to see him again. Maybe his feelings were hurt, and he thought he disappointed you with his stroke game." Carrie's laughter came through the phone, and I honestly couldn't help but laugh with her.

"There ain't no way in hell he would think that." Nope, that wasn't even an option with the way I was moaning and screaming all damn night. He knows exactly what he does to women—what he did to me—so there's no danger of that.

Carrie was silent, which meant she was thinking. A dangerous thing for her. "Then why'd you sneak out the way you did? Why not wake up next to that fine ass man and let him give you one more for the road? I don't understand. You liked him. A lot. Otherwise, you wouldn't have gone upstairs with him. I'm the one who doesn't like to get my feelings involved, but you… you're different. If you ask me, you need to give him a chance."

Everything she said was true, but I also had to acknowledge that just because I wanted something didn't mean I'd get it. Yes, I liked Hunter. Very much. I also know that I have more going on in my life than he's probably used to dealing with. With the way he looked and who he was, I'm sure he had women shooting their shots with him every day. Why would he want to be with a single mother who sometimes had to live paycheck to paycheck? He wouldn't.

But that doesn't change the way he looked at me that night, as if I were the only woman that mattered. That's a heady feeling to have the full attention of Hunter Malone. Those deep blue eyes and that little smirk on his lips. Just remembering the feel of him kissing my bare skin, tasting me in places that had me writing and moaning beneath him. Damn, that man was dangerous to my mental state. I needed to stay as far away from him as I could.

"Carrie. I'm not going." There. I said it.

"Um, what do you mean, you're not going? Hunter wants to see you, and I know you want to see him."

Plating some chicken nuggets for Malachi, I knew I had to stay firm. If I didn't, Carrie would convince me to go out tomorrow. It was only one night, but I had to protect myself from falling into the trap of chasing after a man who only gave the bare minimum. Nope. I wasn't going to do it. "I mean, I'm staying home. I don't want to see Hunter Malone again."

What was that saying about famous last words... Yeah, that.

Seven
Hunter

"What the fuck do you mean, she's not coming?"

Bryce called as I was leaving my last meeting of the day. This was not the news I wanted to hear.

"Bryce, you were supposed to make this happen for me."

It wasn't his job to get my woman for me, but he and I both knew taking the soft approach wasn't always how I did things. Hell, it was never how I did things. Left to me, I'd have stormed into that law office she worked at and made a damn scene as I carried her out with me.

I'd waited a whole week to see her. It had been difficult to not call her. The memory of her voice and the feel of her soft skin wouldn't let me rest at night. Women didn't make me feel this way, but there was something about Anya that I couldn't get out of my head. I should have been able to enjoy my one night with her and move on. Why? Because that's what I did. Women loved me. They loved how I treated them in public and craved how I handled them in private. But when the night was over, so was the connection.

Relationships were for the weak. For men who didn't understand that the world was there for the taking. I could press any number in my phone and have a woman on her knees in front of me in no less than fifteen minutes. That's what I was used to. Doing whatever the fuck pleased me.

Then Anya walked her beautiful ass into my life. Now I'm over here trying to arrange double-dates and shit. This wasn't like me, and I wasn't happy that this is what I was left with.

Bryce was yelling into the phone, but I hadn't heard half of what he said. "Man, you know you come on too strong. Maybe it's time for you to just need to let it go. Not every woman wants to be tamed by the Hunter."

Stepping into my office, I walked over to the large window overlooking downtown Boston. I could have anything and anyone I wanted. So why was this one woman getting to me? I felt my hand rubbing against my chest near my heart. Why did her rejection hurt so much? "Are you sure Carrie said Anya won't be there tonight?"

"Yeah, Carrie just called me. Said it would just be her tonight, that Anya wasn't going to make it. Anyway, I gotta go. I'm not pushing either way, but maybe you should think about letting this one go."

As soon as we hung up, I went to my desk and picked up the piece of paper with her phone number on it that I'd gotten the other day. All I wanted was one more night with her. After that, I'd be over this fascination with Anya and could walk away. I could get back to the life I'd been living before I met her.

Determined to focus on other shit and forget about Anya for a few hours, I stared at the papers on my desk before picking them up. Sighing, I shook my head to clear away the thoughts running through my mind. I had to remember that even when I did see her again, that it would be the last time. It would be much too easy to become addicted to her. I'd want things to continue for longer than they should, even though I know I'm not the kind who did long-term relationships.

Two hours later, I still sat in my office reading over the documentation for a contract worth over ten million dollars. That should have been the only thing on my mind. My entire focus. Turning away from the words that I couldn't seem to process correctly, I propped my feet on my desk and leaned back. My head tilting up to the ceiling, I tried to understand what the fuck was going on with me lately. It was after five, and although it would be an early day for me, I knew it was time for me to head out. I wasn't getting things done as I wanted, and it was a waste of time for me to be here. Since it was Friday night, the bar would be full of beautiful, scantily clad women. If I wanted to, I could find someone to help me forget Anya, at least for the night. Yeah, that's exactly what I should do.

Placing my feet on the floor, I stood from my chair, grabbed my wallet and keys, and walked out of my office. Natalie looked at me in shock, but I ignored her. "See you Monday."

"Um... You're leaving?"

I paused and turned to look at her. "Yes. Is there a problem?" My tone was sharper than usual, but Natalie worked with me for enough years; she knew it wasn't truly directed at her. My mind was filling up with reckless, stupid thoughts, and I needed to do something before I made a damn fool of myself.

Instead of going to The Tower, all I wanted to do was head over to Anya's house. Find out why she didn't come out tonight. Was she really not feeling well? My mind was going down a path it shouldn't, but the thoughts wouldn't stop.

"No. Not a problem at all. See you Monday," she said in an overly sweet tone. Damn, that meant I needed to buy her something to make up for being an ass.

With a nod, I began making my way to the elevator. As soon as the doors closed, I knew I was losing the battle. I wasn't going to do it. There was no way in hell I was going to just show up at a woman's house without advance notice.

What if she had a boyfriend? Then she never should have slept with me last weekend and she needed to be outed.

What if she didn't want to see me again? Not possible. I refuse to even consider the thought.

What if...

You know what? Fuck the what ifs.

Finally making it to the underground garage, I quickly climbed into my car. Decision time. I knew some may consider what I was about to do crossing the line, but I didn't get where I was in life without taking chances. Something inside me was telling me to not give up on Anya. That I needed to understand why I couldn't get her out of my mind. Activating voice calling, I waited for Bryce to pick up the phone.

"I knew your ass would call me back. Whatever you're thinking, just stop."

"Don't tell me what to do," I groused. "What time are you meeting Carrie?"

"In two hours, at seven. Why?"

"Just something I have planned for Anya," I responded.

"She's not going to be there. What could you have planned for her?"

"Just keep Carrie busy and focused on you tonight. Let me focus on what I have for Anya. Did Carrie say if Anya would be home tonight?"

Bryce's sigh came through the line. "Dude! Don't fuck this up for me with Carrie. If you piss off her friend, then I'll probably pay for it later."

"Nah, you'll be good. Just tell me if you know she'll be home tonight," I demanded from my friend as I drove to the Tower.

Low laughter, not the good kind, came through. "Man, I don't know. All Carrie said was Anya wasn't going to be there tonight. Damn, you're such an asshole."

"Yeah, I know." Hanging up the phone, I couldn't help the smile that came over my face. This would be the night I'd finally get over my infatuation with a woman I had no business wanting this much in the first damn place.

Less than twenty minutes later, I stood in my apartment living room as I held my phone in the palm of my hand. I plugged her number into my phone. The message was ready to send. Glancing at the time, I noticed it was just before six o'clock. That gave me more than one hour to set my plan in motion. I know my ego had taken a hit when she'd left without a word, but I wasn't looking for revenge. This was about finishing what we'd started. I hadn't been ready for her to walk away from me. I still wasn't ready. This was the next best option.

A frisson of doubt entered my mind as I thought about her response to what I had planned. But I pushed that shit to the back of my mind. No risk. No reward. Glancing down at the message, I hit send.

Me: Hey Anya, it's me, Hunter.

Delivered... Read.

Staring down at my phone, I waited for her to respond. Setting the device on the dresser, I moved to get undressed and hop in the shower. No more than a minute later, which seemed like a short lifetime, I heard my phone buzz. Picking it up, I read her response.

Anya: Hi Hunter. How'd you get this number?

Oh no, little rabbit. You don't get to set the tone.

Me: I thought you were coming out tonight?

Anya:...

Anya: No. I'm not feeling well, so I'm staying home tonight.

Me: That's unfortunate. Anything you need?

Anya: Thank you. No, I'm good. You have fun tonight.

Me: Don't worry, we will.

Gotcha.

Placing the phone down again, I walked into my large bathroom to get ready for the evening. Someone else might take this as a brush-off, but I wasn't like most people. Never have been. Never will be.

Standing in front of the mirror, I knew what women saw when they looked at me. Tall, blond, blue eyes, wealthy, and I have a big... ego. Being with me was a privilege and an honor, all wrapped up in one. I also knew my personality could either draw people to me or push them away. I rarely gave a fuck what others thought of me.

A self-made millionaire before the age of thirty, and I wasn't planning to stop anytime soon. If someone didn't like how I came across, they had a choice. Accept me as I was or get the fuck out of my way. Usually, people knew it was in their best interest to accept me as is because I would not change my ways for anyone. I was who I was. And tonight, I was going for what I wanted, as I always did.

Glancing down at my phone, I see that I had an alert waiting for me. Reading the message from a woman I'd hooked up with a few months ago, I didn't even read the message before deleting it without a second thought. Anya was the only woman I wanted to focus on right now. Anyone else could wait.

Grabbing my keys, I made my way out of my apartment. Getting to the hallway elevators, I could hear the din from the lobby and bar as people mixed and mingled. On any other Friday night, I would be right in the middle of the fun. Sizing up the women looking for an adventure and selecting one lucky lady for a night of fun and debauchery. But tonight, I had other, more important plans.

Climbing into my car, I pushed the button for the navigation system. Once the address for my intended location was plugged in, I smiled. The night was just beginning, and I couldn't wait for what was about to happen.

Thirty minutes later, I pulled up in front of her small house just outside of Boston. Dialing her number into the phone, it rang three times before she picked up.

"Hello? Hunter?"

"Hey, Anya. How are you feeling?" I asked, but I could see her pacing in front of the living room window.

A pause. Yeah, she was trying to think of the right answer. I'm sure my call caught her off-guard.

"I'm okay. Just wasn't feeling too good earlier. I'll be fine."

"I'm sorry to hear that you're not feeling well." I watched as she paused, placing her head in her hand.

"Hunter?"

"Yeah," I responded, not taking my eyes off the blurry image of her through the window.

"Why are you calling? I mean, you haven't reached out this entire week, then our friends are trying to set us up on a double date with them. Silly, right?"

Glancing behind me at the van pulling up, I knew it was time. Stepping out of my car, I began walking up to her front door. "No. Not silly at all. You left without saying goodbye. I wanted to see you again."

I could hear her sigh. "Let's just get this over with. You and I both know that you're out of my league. I thought I should walk away before you told me to leave. Hunter, it's not a big deal. It's fine. It was fun, but it was time for Cinderella to leave the ball."

My hand poised to knock on her front door when her words clicked. "Wait a minute. You mean to tell me you left because you thought I was going to kick you out? Oh, beautiful little Anya. If only you knew." I'm not gonna try to act like I wouldn't have done that with anyone except her. I had other plans for her that morning, but it was too late to go back in time. All I could do was focus on the here and now. Bringing my hand down, I knocked on the door.

"I'm sorry, Hunter. Someone's at my door. Give me just a second."

"No problem. I'll be here." Removing the phone from my ear, I heard the locks disengage, then a pause. Then the door opened slowly.

"Hunter?" Glancing at her phone, she looked at me with shock on her face. "How did you know where I live?"

Lifting my phone, I ended the call. "I have my ways. Since you weren't in the mood to come out with us tonight, I wanted to bring the night to you." Turning to the two women holding bags of food, I motioned them forward. "Step back, sweetheart. I've brought dinner."

"Wait. What?"

Her tone was filled with shock and surprise, which I understood. But I also needed her to move so I could set the food up.

"Step back, Anya."

"Um," she had a look of panic on her face.

"Mommy? What you doin'?"

My gaze shifted down to the tiny voice I'd just heard. What the hell? I took an initial step back as a little brown face peaked around Anya's legs. A child. She has a child.

Well, fuck me.

Eight
Anya

Was I really on the phone talking to Hunter Malone?

Why did he care if I'd eaten dinner?

I mean, sure, I'd lied through my damn teeth about not feeling well. I felt fine, but I had to say something to explain why I wouldn't go out with them tonight. Telling Carrie or Hunter that I didn't want to be around him because I was afraid of how I'd respond was not an option. The man did something to me that I didn't want to examine. So, yes, I was afraid the longer I was in his presence, the more I would be unable to walk away unscathed. There was no way in hell I was going to become a woman who couldn't let go of a man, even if all the signs were there.

That I wanted to climb into his bed again and not leave until my legs turned into wet noodles didn't seem like the best thing to say to anyone. Hell, I didn't even say that out loud to myself. Those were the silent thoughts I kept to myself until I was alone.

Plus, I was a responsible mother with a small child. I couldn't be out here bed-hopping with some guy. No matter how sexy he was or how well-known or wealthy. But why was he calling me? Plus, he still hadn't said how he got my number. Then again, I'd told him my full name, so I'm positive it wasn't that difficult to find. It made sense, but still...

"Hunter?"

"Yeah," he responded through the other line.

God, his voice was like molasses on a warm day. I could feel my body responding to his voice, wanting more, but knowing I needed to stay far away. "Why are you calling? I mean, you hadn't reached out this entire week. Then our friends are trying to set us up on a double date with them. Silly, right?"

"No. Not silly at all. You left without saying goodbye. I wanted to see you again."

Could this really be happening? Did he want to see me again? Maybe I'd made the wrong decision about leaving his apartment. I turned to look at myself in the mirror, critical of the image staring back at me. It was ridiculous of me to think this way. I'm sure he was just being friendly. Or maybe he was trying to connect for a booty call.

Either way, I'm not sure why he was so determined to see me. The one thing I was sure of was that I couldn't afford to fall down this rabbit hole. "Let's just get this over with. You and I both know that you're out of my league. I thought I should walk away before you told me to leave. Hunter, it's fine. It was fun, but it was time for Cinderella to leave the ball."

He was silent for a moment before his voice burst out. "Wait a minute. You mean to tell me you left because you thought I was going to kick you out? Oh, beautiful little Anya. If only you knew."

There was a knock at my door. Glancing at the clock, I noticed it was just before seven o'clock. I wasn't expecting anyone tonight. I'd planned for a quiet dinner and some kid shows with my little guy. The knock sounded again. "I'm sorry, Hunter. Someone's at my door. Give me just a second."

"No problem. I'll be here."

Once at the door, I looked out the peephole and froze. Glancing down at my phone, I looked again. My eyes must be playing tricks on me because it sure as hell looked as if

Hunter were standing outside my door. "What the hell is happening?" I whispered to myself.

Flipping the locks, I took a deep breath and slowly opened the door. Coming face-to-face with the one man I never thought I'd see again. "Hunter?" I glanced down at my phone, then up at him again. My gaze couldn't seem to leave him. Hunter stood in front of me wearing a blue shirt, dark jeans, with his hair twisted up into a messy bun. A vision of me running my hands through the thick strands as he thrust inside my body came to my mind. I could feel my eyes glaze over as I recalled the feel of his body sliding against mine as he twisted me in ways that had my body hurting so good for days after.

I asked the first question that came into my head. "How did you know where I live?"

He smirked before answering. "I have my ways. Since you weren't in the mood to come out with us tonight, I wanted to bring the night to you." He then turned to look over his shoulder and motioned to some people with bags. "Step back, sweetheart. I've brought dinner."

"Wait. What?" Did this man really bring food to my house without asking? I didn't even give him my address, so all this was out of bounds.

"Step back, Anya."

Not sure why I did it, but I shifted a bit to the side to let the women with food enter the house.

"Mommy? What you doin'?" Malachi called out to me and I jumped at least a foot in the air. How could I forget my baby was standing right there beside me? This is what happened when I focused on the wrong damn thing.

"Yes, baby. The nice man brought you and mommy dinner. Are you hungry?" I was too busy looking at my son, so I wasn't looking at

Hunter's face. However, I heard the shock in his voice.

"You have a son?"

Glancing up at him, I took in the look on his face and shook my head. Here we go. I know how this goes. I meet a man, I think there may be something there, they find out I have a son, and suddenly they remember something else they needed to do.

"I do." I paused, staring at him as he stared down at my son. "Did you suddenly remember a prior engagement?"

His gaze tracked to mine, but I dared not look away. It disappointed me that he was responding this way. Then again, better for me to know now, rather than find out down the road. Some men didn't want to deal with a woman who had a child. I get it. Hell, one man even said women with children were damaged goods, but that since I was so fine, he'd make an exception for me. Yeah, I left that disaster of a date within seconds of him finishing that statement.

"No. I don't have a prior engagement," he said, finally looking up into my face. "I'm afraid there may not be any kid-friendly food in those bags."

Glancing down at Malachi, then up at Hunter, I nodded. "Understandable. I mean, you came over expecting one thing. Instead, you got something completely different."

"Maybe I should have made sure I had all my facts first," he said with a furrow on his brow.

Well, this blows. I wanted to slam the door in his face, but I held off. If I were honest, I knew I didn't tell him about Malachi when we met last week for a reason. My child isn't usually the first topic of conversation when I'm out at night. It's just that if I'm out having fun and enjoying myself, I hold a piece of me back. Namely, that I have a three-year-old son waiting for me at home. If I continue to see someone beyond a first date, which doesn't happen often, I let them know about Malachi. They would need to understand that I have responsibilities at home. I won't let anything, or anyone, get in the way of that. Getting back to the conversation at hand, I nodded. "Well, you seemed to get some important information about me, but I understand what you mean."

"Is he your real reason for not coming tonight?" He motioned to Malachi.

His tone wasn't nasty, but I wasn't sure I liked the insinuation. "No," I snapped. "Listen, thank you for dinner, but you stopped by unannounced. I'd planned for my son and me to have a movie night. I still don't even know how you got my address. Actually, everything about this situation is just odd." I looked over my shoulder at the two women standing next to the table. "And why are those two women still standing in my kitchen?"

Hunter cleared his throat. "Well, they were going to serve us dinner. I didn't know how you'd feel about being alone with me in your home. I mean, you're right, I did show up unannounced," he said with a small smile. "I hired these women to help us tonight and to make you feel a bit safer."

"You..." I glanced over my shoulder at the women, who offered soft smiles, but otherwise said nothing. "You brought them because you wanted me to feel safe?"

"Mommy? Nuggets?" Malachi said again, pulling on my shirt. His little body was hidden behind mine, all except for his head. He stared up at Hunter, who must have looked like a giant to my little boy.

"No, I don't think there are any chicken nuggets, baby."

Hunter shifted. "Well, there may not be any nuggets in there, but I have some fried chicken. I didn't know what kind of food you liked, so I bought a little bit of everything. Lasagna. Chicken. Salmon. Plus, there were side dishes to go with everything."

"You thought of everything, didn't you?"

He took a step closer. "I try my best."

My eyes widened at him. "What are you doing? I thought you were leaving?"

Hunter smiled down at me. His eyes captured mine, holding me frozen under his watchful gaze. "Who said I was going anywhere? I came here to check on you. If you recall, you told me you weren't feeling well. I brought you dinner because I was concerned you hadn't eaten."

"I know you were expecting a two-person party." Yeah, I knew this was a booty-call covered up to look like a wellness check. I was crazy, not stupid.

"Now that it's a three-person gathering, and that makes it even better. So," he nodded towards the room behind me, "Are you going to let me in so we can eat?"

Even after all this, it took me a few more seconds to decide. I glanced over at the wait staff standing in my kitchen, down at Malachi who was eyeing the food on the table, and then back to Hunter, who stood there looking like a modern-day Viking God.

"Sure, come on in," I said, waving him inside. "You'll have to excuse the mess. I wasn't really expecting company tonight."

He stepped inside, glancing around my home as if memorizing the space. "I'm the one intruding. Plus, if you haven't been feeling well, you wouldn't have been worrying about picking up a stray toy or two."

Turning to him, I put a hand on my hip. "Okay, fine. You know I wasn't sick."

He nodded. "I know. You were avoiding me. What I was to know is, why?"

I wasn't ready to answer that question for him, so I ignored it. "Well, let's not have all this good food go to waste. Please take a seat." Cringing at my tone, I recognized the hysteria bubbling up to the surface.

"I'm hungry, Mommy." Malachi looked up at me with large, brown eyes. Grabbing his hand, I began walking us over to the kitchen table.

"You can run, but you can't hide. I'll get the answers to my questions, Anya," I heard Hunter say as he walked beside me. Once we got to the table, he stood next to a chair, waiting and watching.

Ignoring the large man standing in my dining room, I picked up my son and placed him in his booster seat at the table. I moved to make a plate for him when Hunter motioned with his hand. "Relax. These ladies are here to do that for us tonight. Let's just relax and enjoy the evening."

I glanced at him and then at the ladies, then back to Hunter. "You like getting your way, don't you?"

"Always," he said before glancing at the ladies waiting to serve dinner. "Ladies, feel free to serve the little man first."

Oh, this motherfucker is good. Shit. I think I may be in trouble.

Nine
Hunter

I know showing up at Anya's house was presumptuous. When Bryce told me her excuse for not showing up tonight, I knew I was going to do something to break through her barriers. She was hiding from me, and I wanted to know why. What I didn't expect was for her to have a child. Did I care? Not really. Was this unexpected situation going to change anything? Hell no. I want to know her better, so that's what I'm going to do. Child or no child.

Yeah, okay. Maybe I needed to adjust my approach just a little. I'd never dated a woman with a child before. Did he still wear diapers, or could he go to the bathroom by himself? Although I'd heard him speak a few words, was that all he could say? Glancing at the table, I looked at the food displayed, most of which were meant for humans over the age of ten. Plus, he was so young, which brought another thought to my mind.

"Where's his father?" Tact had never been a skill of mine.

Anya stopped fussing with her son and looked over at me. Her gaze was intense. Challenging me. Not many people did that. Especially women. They'd usually lower their gaze, but not Anya. Leaning back, her eyes still focused on my face, I noticed her lips tilt up in a crooked smile.

"Why?"

Because I want to make sure I don't have any competition. "Just curious. I'm trying to get to know you better."

"I'm still trying to understand how you know where I lived."

I glanced over at her son, who was gobbling up his meal, not paying the adults any attention. "You can trust me. You know who I am. It's not like I can hide."

"Hunter, you showed up at my home." I could hear the strain in her voice as she glanced at her son.

"With two women who can serve as chaperones for us. Listen, I didn't know you had a son. If my showing up here upset you, that wasn't my intention. But I also won't apologize for doing it. You were avoiding me, and I wanted to see you again. I did what I felt was the next best option. I came to you on your own turf."

"You know that's not how regular people do things. We don't have secret ways of finding out where people live and showing up with a full course dinner in tow, with servers."

I smiled. "What can I say? I do things my own way." Leaning forward, I placed my elbows on the table. "It's okay to be happy that I'm here," I said with a wink.

Her eyes widened before she looked down at her plate of food. She spooned some potatoes into her mouth, delaying her response to me. Her tactics did not fool me, so I smiled in her direction as she avoided my gaze. If she truly wasn't happy to have me here, she would have stopped me from coming in. And no matter how much I would have wanted to stay, if she'd pushed me out or denied me, I wouldn't have forced myself inside. At least, I don't think I would have. It's a good thing we didn't have to test that theory.

I took a sip of red wine, enjoying the smoothness of the liquid. "So, now that I'm here and we have this lovely dinner, tell me something about you that I don't know."

A week ago, when we'd first met, we talked about the superficial things. The stuff you tell a first date because you're not sure how deep you want to go. I want to know more about Anya. What makes her tick? What makes her smile? What makes her cry? She was an enigma to me. I wanted to understand why I couldn't get her off my mind. My nights were full of memories of our night together. I spent my days thinking about how and when I could see her again. I wasn't the type to do relationships, so I needed to figure out this unending infatuation with Anya. If that meant spending more time with her, then that's what I was going to do.

As she glanced up at me, I couldn't help but think about how beautiful she was. No make-up. Casual clothes. Hair a tad messy, which is not something I was going to mention to her. Without even trying to, she looked natural and beautiful, and I wanted her even more.

After a few moments of staring at me, she nodded. "What is it you want to know?" Turning to her son, she shook her head. "No, Malachi. Eat your vegetables," she chastised him lightly.

"No veg'bles, momma!"

I almost laughed at the mutinous look on his face. However, I was also a very smart man and knew finding humor in the little guy's rebellion was not the best way to make a good impression on Anya. Instead, I picked up a few of the green beans on my plate and ate them. Anya saw what I did and jumped on it.

"Malachi, if you eat your vegetables, you'll get big and strong like Mr. Hunter. Don't you want to be big and strong? Eat just a few more vegetables. If you do, then you can have more chicken."

I'd only been with them for less than an hour, but she seemed like a wonderful mother. If I were honest with myself, I knew that I'd come over to her place expecting Anya would be free for me to do what I do best. Fuck her, then leave.

Now, I needed to rethink my approach. She and her son were a package deal. Glancing over at her tiny human as he chewed one green bean extremely slowly, I couldn't help but smile at the dejected look on his face. The food was terrific, but to a small child, anything green was the opposite of good.

"You never answered my question," I interjected.

"Which question was that?"

My gaze bored into hers. "You know which question. Is his father around?"

Her mouth dropped open, and she stared at me for a moment. "Um. No, he's not. I mean, he sends support, but he has no interest in being a father. I'm okay with how things worked out, because Malachi and I are doing fine."

"A man should want to be there for his son," I groused. While I understood that not every relationship or marriage was like my parents, the thought that a father would choose not to be in his son's life did not sit right with me one bit.

She nodded as she chewed a last bite of her food. "Yeah, well, some men don't feel the same way you do."

"Were you married?" I asked. Not that it mattered, but I was on a mission.

"No."

I nodded in response. At that moment, I knew I was spiraling down a rabbit hole that I shouldn't. I'd only spent one night with her. There was no way I should be feeling this connection to her. Then again, that argument went out the window when I called Conall to find out her address. It wasn't like she was the only woman in the world, but she was the only woman who caught my attention this way. The only woman I'd gone out of my way to see again. Living in Bachelor Tower, as it was fondly referred to, allowed me to have access to any number of women. Ones who would gladly give me all the attention they thought I needed. That's why it was so telling that I was here, chasing after a woman who'd tried to deny me.

"Excuse me, Mr. Malone," one server interrupted my thoughts. "Would you like dessert now?"

Glancing over at Anya and Malachi, whose eyes were focused on the cake sitting on the counter, I nodded. "As long as Anya and Malachi are ready."

"I really shouldn't," Anya said, her eyes glazing over as she stared at the treat.

"Cake!" Malachi yelled out.

"He's going to have me up all night." She turned to look at me. "This food is so good. Malachi's gonna expect food like this all the time now. I think you may have created a little food monster."

I hadn't expected things to go this way tonight, but even I must admit that I was happy with how everything was happening. "Well, I'm happy to make sure he gets his wish. You're never too young to enjoy the things you want. Your little guy simply knows what he likes." At my nod, the ladies began removing the dinner plates just before cutting and serving dessert. They even pulled out a carafe of coffee.

"Ma'am, would you like some coffee?"

A smile came over Anya's face. "Yes, please."

"Coffee, Sir?"

I nodded in response, but my gaze never left Anya's face. She truly was beautiful. I know bringing dinner over like this, with servers, was a bit over the top. But I'm glad I did. It worked out better than I could have imagined. As we sipped our coffee, Malachi shoveled cake into his tiny mouth.

"Slow down, Malachi," Anya said as she softly grabbed his chin, using a napkin to wipe some of the chocolate from his face. "You're gonna get a tummy ache. Smaller bites, okay?"

"Yes, momma."

As I watched the scene play out in front of me, I knew I'd made the right decision tonight. "I want to see you again."

Her movements paused. Glancing at the servers, Malachi, the floor, Anya looked anywhere and everywhere, except at me.

"Why?"

Now that was the ultimate question. "Look at me, Anya." I waited a few seconds as her eyes flitted over toward the servers, who were busy with their duties. Her eyes landed on my face and I felt a smile come over my face. "I want to see you again because you intrigue me."

She released a small laugh as she shook her head. "This is all upside down and backward."

"Doesn't matter how we started," I countered. "All that matters is where we go from here."

"I'm a single mother," she reminded me. As if I could forget, especially when proof of her status was staring at me with wide eyes from his booster seat.

The smile that came over my face couldn't be helped. "Yeah, I figured that out already. Are you not allowed to date because you're a single mother?" I would not allow her room to make any excuses. Anya's face was serious, and for a moment... just a moment, I felt unsure of what her answer would be.

"Of course, I can date. You should ask yourself if dating a single mother is something you want, even casually. What happened last week," she paused, glancing over at the ladies clearing away the catering dishes from the meal, "isn't like me. I spend most of my time at work and with my son. I'm a legal secretary at a job I enjoy and that pays the bills. This," she used one hand to motion towards the women, "isn't something I'm used to. My life is simple. Easy. Boring. Everything I do has to factor in Malachi."

"What, momma?" Hearing his name, the little boy in question entered the conversation.

She smiled at her little boy. "Nothing, honey. I love you."

"Love you," he responded just as quickly, his focus once again on the cake in front of him.

Left with no other choice, I nodded in response to her words. "I hear you. Anya, the one thing I can guarantee is that I'm not here to pressure you. I just want to make my intentions clear. Seeing you again is what I want. If you want that too, we'll make it work for us." Seeing the ladies were all done with getting everything cleared up, I placed my hands on the table and stood. "I think it's time for me to head out. Thank you for welcoming me into your home and at your table."

She stood as well. "I should thank you for bringing dinner. I know you probably expected…."

I interrupted. "No, I wasn't expecting anything other than a nice dinner with a beautiful woman. That's it. Nothing more." Expectations and desires were two vastly different things. "That you allowed me in and didn't tell me to never come back was a gift. From an early age, I learned to always take the gift when offered."

She stared up at me, her beautiful brown eyes. I wanted to lean down and capture her soft lips with mine. Just standing here with her made my cock thicken in my pants. *Slow down, buddy.* I was smart enough to know that dinner didn't mean I should expect anything, but I sure as fuck wanted her underneath me.

"Down, momma." Malachi's voice broke through the tension hovering in the air.

Glancing over at the little guy was like a cold-ass shower. I took a step back from Anya before addressing the ladies waiting to exit. "Thank you, ladies." Walking over to them, I pulled out my wallet and provided them both with a generous tip on top of the one already provided to their company. "Exceptional service, as usual."

"Thank you, Sir. Have a great night. Ma'am," they addressed Anya before heading out.

"Hunter," I heard Anya call out to me. I turned to see Malachi toddling over to his toys piled up in the corner. My gaze slid to her. Her hands were twisting and fidgeting. "Yes. I want to see you again."

"That's what I'd hoped you'd say."

Ten
Hunter

If I've learned anything over these past two weeks, it's that the best-laid plans could go haywire from one moment to the next. I'd been trying to see Anya alone for over ten days straight. Unfortunately, here I was on the eleventh day and it wasn't looking any better.

Nothing was happening the way I wanted. It was beyond frustrating. If it wasn't business meetings and last-minute negotiations getting in the way, Anya couldn't find a sitter for Malachi, or it was too late to even ask her to try.

I guess this is what she meant when warning me that dating a single mother was different.

Since I'd never been in this situation before, I probably wasn't handling it the best way I could have. Now, sitting here in my office overlooking the Charles River, questions were swirling around in my head. I didn't like the direction of my thoughts. After meeting Anya, I knew I wanted to see her again. I wanted to be with her again. Thinking over the voicemail she left me tonight, I needed to really think about what this change might mean for me.

I wasn't someone who was used to being questioned. I went after the things I wanted. That's just how I operated. Permission was something other people asked for. I took. I demanded. People bent to my will, not the other way around. This is why I knew I had a decision to make about how I wanted things to progress.

Sure, I'd seen Anya over the past two weeks, but a quick lunch here or dinner there wasn't my idea of how this relationship should be progressing. I was already frustrated as hell, and now this. How the hell was I supposed to respond? Wasn't this supposed to be easy?

Find a woman I like.

Date that woman.

Get that woman in my bed.

Move on from that woman.

Yet, every time I thought about moving on from Anya, something inside me seized up. No, things weren't progressing the way I wanted them to, but breaking things off with her didn't sit right with me either. Even with trying to schedule some time to see each other alone and my business getting in the way, I knew having her in my life was what I wanted. What I needed.

And with that thought came another realization. If that were the case, why was I fighting this so damn hard? I closed my eyes as I thought about her message.

I know this isn't what you signed up for.

It was too damn late for her to have second thoughts about us. She was in my life now, and I would not give her up just because things weren't neat and tidy, presented to me with a red bow on top.

I need to think of Malachi. If we're going to be together, you must be all in.

Hadn't I shown her how much I wanted this?

Maybe we should stop trying to fool ourselves. Maybe this won't work after all.

I thought about how I'd allowed everything under the sun to come between us seeing each other these past two weeks. Spending some actual quality time with each other, beyond some stolen moments here and there, had been placed on the back-burner. I had to pause at the thought. If I were genuinely

137

trying to give it my all, then I'd be with her right now. Instead, I was standing in my office about to go into another unnecessary meeting. I didn't need to be here for this. I could trust my number two to handle this, but something was holding me back from letting go. My company was my first love and for many years, had been my only love. Letting someone else run the show on my behalf wasn't something I was ready to do. Okay, maybe not just yet. But I also needed to find the balance because having Anya in my life was non-negotiable.

"Fuck this," I said out loud to my empty office.

Grabbing my keys and wallet, I walked out into the main hallway. Going to my Chief Operating Officer's door, I stepped inside without knocking. "Dan, I need you to handle the meeting tonight." Dan looked at me with something like shock on his face. Was he really that damn surprised?

"Sure, Hunter. I have everything I need. Everything good?"

"I need to leave. Can you handle the meeting without me or not?" I growled. The man was ivy league educated and paid a very handsome salary to handle the shit I asked him to do. There was no reason to act as if he'd never had an ounce of responsibility, even if I gave it to him in tiny increments.

Dan nodded. "Of course, I can. It's just... actually, never mind. Yes, I got this. We've discussed how you want this deal to play out."

"Good." I turned to leave, but paused and faced him again. "Thank you."

Dan's face immediately flushed red as he stammered. "You're welcome, Hunter. Thank you for entrusting me with this meeting. I won't let you down."

I stared at him for a beat longer before nodding once. "Make sure that you don't."

Making my way out of the space and into
the elevator, I took a deep breath. This was a
turning point for me. I could admit to being
nervous about what this meant for me. Pulling
out my phone, I listened to Anya's message one
more time.

"*Hey, Hunter. I know you're busy right
now, but I needed to call. I know this isn't what
you signed up for. Dating a single mom can be
frustrating and difficult, and sometimes my
time is not my own. Don't get me wrong, I've
enjoyed all the time we've spent together, even
the brief moments.*" She paused. I knew exactly
what was coming next because I'd listened to
the message several times. "*Malachi keeps
asking about you. He wants to know when he'll
see you again, and I don't know what to tell
him. I know you said you wanted to see what
could happen between us and that my son
wasn't a problem. But let's be real, I think it is.
And that's okay. But I need to be honest with*

you. Settling for half of someone is not okay with me. Nor do I want that for my son. I need to think of Malachi. If we're going to be together, you must be all in. If you're not willing or able to do that, then we need to stop doing this. Maybe we should stop trying to fool ourselves. Maybe this won't work after all."

Listening to her words for the fifth time still didn't make them any easier to hear. Climbing into my vehicle, I called her as soon as I pulled out of the garage. The phone rang four times before her voicemail came on. "Anya, I'm on my way. I want you and Malachi to pack a bag because we're going away for the weekend. No arguments or discussions. Call your office and let them know you won't be in tomorrow or the next day. Tell them whatever you need, just be ready to go away with me. I'll be there in thirty."

Disconnecting the call, I smiled for the first time since I'd picked up her voicemail. It was time for me to make my intentions known. I was not prepared to give up my bachelor status, but I was ready to see how things would progress with Anya. I needed to put some other things in motion for this weekend, so I made a few more phone calls as I made my way to her home.

Pulling up to her house, I noticed Anya must have just arrived as well, since she was pulling some bags from the trunk. Parking behind her, I stepped out of my vehicle and walked up to her. She turned to me; her expression closed. "I got your message," I said, grabbing the bags from her arms.

"It wasn't meant to make you feel guilty, or that you had to rush over here. I just wanted you to know that I understood. You thought you were getting a carefree, single woman who was full of fun and sexy times."

"Who said you aren't full of fun and sexy times?"

She gave me a small smile. "You know what I mean."

I chose instead to ignore her attempts to push me away. Nodding my head towards the front door, I began walking. "Come on, let's go inside." Once I stepped over the threshold, I heard Malachi call out to me.

"Hunter!" His little body barreled in my direction. Quickly setting the bags down, I grabbed up the little tyke just before he crashed into my legs.

"Malachi!" I threw him up in the air. His squeals and laughter were loud but welcome. How could I have put business in front of these two? It had been two days since I'd come over for dinner with them because of company obligations. Anya said Malachi had been asking about me, but maybe I needed to see him as well. "Hey, buddy."

"Hi, Hunter. Hungry?"

When was this little guy ever not hungry? "Yes, I'm hungry."

"Chicken nuggets?" And there were the puppy dog eyes. I tried not to get in the middle of his food requests, especially since I realized he asked for chicken nuggets every night. But the little tyke was clever. He must have a radar that let him know when adults were about to cave in. He always started with the eyes, then the bottom lip would push out, then he used the magic words. "Pweaze, Hunter." That he still couldn't say the letter "L" was kinda cute. I'd never admit it out loud, but the little guy had me wrapped around his tiny fingers. Fighting my need to be around him and his mother was a battle I was happy to lose.

"Oh no you don't, buster. I told you tonight was pasta," Anya interjected. She stood in front of us with her arms crossed.

"Momma. Hunter wants chicken nuggets." Then the little manipulator raised his hands to grab my face. "Hunter? Chicken nuggets?"

"I'm not doing this with you today, Malachi."

She turned that mother's gaze to me, putting me on notice that I'd better not contradict her. That look was something I'd seen before from my own mother. I wanted to laugh because even at her most frustrated and attempts to be stern with her son, my only thought was to pull her into my arms and kiss those soft, plump lips. But I needed to stay in her good graces, so I chose a better option. "I'm happy to eat whatever your momma makes for me."

"Hunter, you have to stop giving him whatever he wants," she sighed, hands on her hips.

Shaking my head, I looked to the side of Malachi, over at Anya staring at us. "I don't give him whatever he wants."

Actually, yes, I do. Last weekend, he wanted to go to the zoo. It took me twenty-four hours to arrange for us to have the entire place to ourselves. I mean, there would be strangers there if I hadn't. Since Malachi was Anya's son, I needed to make sure he was safe. It wasn't that I was beginning to care about the little guy. I wasn't a man who wanted children or a family. In fact, I usually ran in the other direction when the topic came up. With the life I lead, having a family wasn't something I expected to have. It was never part of the future I envisioned for myself. Then again, while I was seeing Anya, I wanted to make sure her son knew just how important he was. They were a package deal, and I was okay with that.

"Hunter, you're spoiling him," Anya said with a firmer tone.

When I glanced up at her, I noticed the smile on her face, so I knew I wasn't in trouble. "Did you pick up my message?"

She shook her head while she unloaded the bags. "No. I saw that you called, but I couldn't pick up. Malachi was having a moment. Plus..." she paused, "I wasn't sure I wanted to hear it."

"Why? Because of that unnecessary message you left for me? Were you trying to break it off?" I placed Malachi on the ground. "Malachi, give your momma and me a few minutes. Can you go play with your toys?"

"Okay, Hunter," he said with a smile before running to his room.

"Answer me, Anya. Were you trying to break things off?" I walked up behind her, wrapping my arms around her waist. She went stiff for a few seconds before leaning back against me.

"I don't want to break things off. But I felt things were off, and I don't want you to feel obligated. You had a whole life before you met me. The women you dated before aren't like me.

I just want you to be sure that this is what you want."

I turned her around so that I could look at her face as I spoke. "I know these past couple of weeks have been hectic, but nothing has changed. I want to be with you." I leaned down, capturing her lips in a kiss. When she shifted, coming to the balls of her feet to press closer, I deepened our connection. I hadn't been inside her since our night in my apartment, but this weekend was going to change all that. Breaking apart, I raised my hands to her face and gripped her tightly. "We're going away for the weekend. We'll leave first thing in the morning."

Anya immediately began shaking her head. "I can't. Malachi—"

"Will be coming with us. I have a friend who owns a vacation house in Martha's Vineyard. I'd like us to go there for the weekend. They use a nanny service that they've vetted and used for years. I've contacted them about having someone to help us with Malachi for the weekend."

She pulled back with an annoyed look on her face. "You called them and made arrangements without me? You can't do that, Hunter. I need to vet them. I need to make sure they're reputable."

Before she finished speaking, I pulled out my phone and dialed a number. "This is Hunter Malone. Yes, we spoke just a few minutes ago. Hold on." I handed the phone over to Anya. "The owner of the agency is on the line. Ask her whatever you want. I've had my security team run a background check on the company and the owner. I've also had my CFO make a few calls to investigate their financials and their business reputation. Talk to her. Ask whatever you want. I'm going to help Malachi pack."

She took the phone, but her eyes were shooting fire. Damn, that was hot.

"Has anyone ever said no to you?"

"Not since I was fourteen." I nodded toward the phone. "Time's wasting. Talk to her. Make sure you're comfortable. The other material has already been sent to me, and you can look at it afterward." I began walking away. Was I overbearing and presumptuous? Abso-fucking-lutely. But I was also determined to make the weekend special, and nothing was going to get in the way of that.

Eleven
Anya

Now, this is what I'm talking about. Before meeting Hunter, nothing like this would have happened to me. Yet, here I was, relaxing on a chaise lounge, a glass of wine in my hand, an e-reader in my hand, and a beautiful breeze flowing over my skin. I admit, when Hunter showed up at my house making demands about us going away for the weekend, I thought he was out of his mind.

That he knew my primary concern would be Malachi broke me down. After speaking with the owner of the nanny service, they eased all my concerns. Well, most of them anyway. He was still too damn bossy for his own good, but I recognized that he was trying to be what I wanted.

I still struggled with believing he wanted to be with me. Models with blonde or flaming red hair and porcelain skin seemed more his type. Not brown-skinned women with a bit too much junk in the trunk and a sassy mouth. Yet here we are.

Only two hours had passed since we'd arrived. Walking into the house, I couldn't help my jaw from falling to the ground. The foyer was almost bigger than my living room. A spiral staircase was off to the side, ascending to the second floor. An extensive library was to the left of me, while a large living area was on the right. The kitchen was located at the back of the house. There seemed to be an entire staff of people inside. The two ladies with Hunter when he brought dinner to my house that first night were waiting inside. I greeted them with a large smile and a small wave.

When Hunter placed his hand on the small of my back, I almost jumped out of my skin. This was the type of place he had access to at a moment's notice? I'm sure the shock was visible on my face, but he was nice enough not to mention it. Our luggage had apparently been taken up to our room. Well, suites, to be exact. My room was a mini apartment with two bedrooms inside. One for me. One for Malachi.

"I thought you'd feel better having him close by. The nanny has to enter the suite to get to Malachi, so you still have complete control," Hunter assured me as we walked into the large space.

"Thank you," my voice was shaky as I responded.

"I want to make sure you're comfortable here with me. There's a staff of about six people who'll be here with us the entire time. Some I paid for. Some paid for by the owner of the house and who live here full-time."

"The ladies from the other night when you brought dinner to my house. Are they on your staff?"

"Not full-time, but I know the owner of the company they work for. Since you responded so well to having them with us the other night, I thought seeing some familiar faces would help."

I nodded. He was right. The stress and nerves had been overtaking me until I saw their faces. For some reason, seeing them helped calm me. They knew me. I knew them. "You thought of everything."

"That's my job," he whispered, wrapping his arms around my waist. "This weekend is for us. You, me, and Malachi. Our time to just relax, have fun, and explore what's happening."

I pulled back, looking into his eyes as he spoke. "Wait. So, you're gonna take time off

from work? A whole day? Unheard of."
Although I had a smile on my face, we both
knew there was some truth to what I was
saying.

Leaning down, he kissed me softly on the
lips, "For you. It's worth it."

"Momma! Hunter! Go play!" Malachi's
voice broke the tension swirling within the
room, and I pulled away from Hunter. The
nanny had been waiting for us when we pulled
up to the house.

"Ma'am. There are some clean children's
bathing suits in the pool room. He could use one
of those if you didn't bring one for him."

Sarah was a college student who worked
for the agency. I'd looked over her credentials
and had a long discussion with the agency
owner before agreeing to speak with her about
helping me with Malachi this weekend. From
everything I'd read and the conversations, she
was one of the best. Clients asked her to return

time and time again. Sometimes, clients got into a bidding war for her services because she was so good with kids and fit in with their families.

"Thanks, Sarah. I brought one with us. Since I wasn't sure, I think I have a bit of everything in his suitcase. I'll get him changed, and we'll come right down."

"Yes, ma'am. I'll be in the kitchen when you're ready."

I turned back to Hunter. "Where's your room?"

He motioned with his head. "Across the hall. I didn't want to be too far away from you and Malachi, but I also didn't want to overstep."

Gawd, could he get any fucking better? "You don't want to be in the same bed with me?" I was teasing, of course, but his blue eyes turned stormy as he looked at me.

"Oh, you can bet your sweet ass I want to be with you. I'm trying to be a better man,

Anya. What we have, what I'm trying to build with you, is different from what I've had with other women. There should be no doubt in that beautiful mind of yours of how I feel about you."

If it weren't the middle of the day and my son wasn't looking at us with those big eyes, probably wondering why we were hugged up on each other, I'd jump him right here and now. "As long as you know the feeling is mutual." I smiled up at him before turning to Malachi. "Are you ready for the beach?"

"Yes," he whisper-yelled before running into the bedroom where he'd be sleeping.

Shifting back to Hunter, I leaned up on my toes. "Thank you for doing this. It means a lot to me." Taking the initiative, I captured his lips with mine. I know how busy he is. Both of us are. But it meant something special to me that he took the time to bring us here. To get away from all the things that get in the way of us seeing each other. He broke the kiss as we both heard Malachi call out my name.

"I'll be done in ten minutes. The staff can unpack for you."

That's something I wasn't used to. "I can unpack for us later."

He shook his head at me. "Sweetheart, let the staff do their job. It's okay. I want you to focus all your time and attention on me and Malachi."

"Will you be able to do the same?" I know it probably seemed out of the blue, but during these past few weeks, getting to know Hunter, I know how often he's pulled in different directions.

"That's the plan. But I can't do that if we're standing here talking about it. Ten minutes, sweetheart."

Now, as I lay here on the lounger, watching Hunter and Malachi play on the beach and build sandcastles, I can appreciate why he brought us here. In Boston, our lives are so wrapped up in our day-to-day activities, I'm not sure if we'd ever get time alone like this. Getting away from it all was probably the best thing for us. Building something with Hunter is what I wanted. Then again, I couldn't shy away from the sliver of negative thoughts running through my head.

If I couldn't be honest with myself, who could I be honest with?

Hunter had been a bachelor for so long. Was he truly ready to give all that up to be with me? To step into a relationship where my responsibilities included a precocious three-year-old boy who had more energy than ten puppies. What if he realized this wasn't what he wanted? That we weren't what he wanted? Could I go back to my everyday life of details? Malachi and I had been fine on our own for so long, and I'm sure I could do that again. The question is, do I want to?

So caught up in my thoughts, I didn't see Hunter approaching.

"What are you over here thinking about?" His deep voice broke through my internal musings.

"Hey," I said, the tone of my voice borderline hysterical. "What?"

He said down on the lounger next to me. "I asked what you were thinking about. Malachi and I have been calling you for five minutes. You were completely zoned out."

Not ready to share all my thoughts, I brushed it off. "Oh, nothing. It's just been a long time since I truly relaxed. This feels nice."

He stared at me as if he knew that wasn't the truth. I looked at him as he sat in front of me and couldn't help but admire his form. Of course, I'd seen him naked before, but not like this. His body was sculpted like a God. His blond hair was slicked back, and water droplets shined like diamonds on his chest. Hunter wasn't over hairy, but his chest had just the right amount. I loved running my fingers over the silky-smooth strands resting along his muscled chest. For a man who worked in an office all day, I still hadn't figured out how he kept himself in such great shape. I asked him about it once, and he told me it was because of his genes and great metabolism. I call bullshit on that, but I kept my thoughts to myself since I have no proof otherwise.

"If you keep looking at me like that, I'm going to ask Sarah to take over while we go inside to my bedroom," Hunter growled out.

Embarrassed that I was caught ogling his body, my eyes shot up to his. "Can you blame me? Have you looked at yourself lately?"

He looked across the landscape, his gaze resting on Sarah and Malachi playing a game of tag in the sand. A smile came over his face, and my heart melted at the sight. I knew fairy tales weren't real, but I hoped like hell this was my chance to get close. When his gaze swung back to me, my breath caught in my chest. The look of desire in his eyes stopped me cold and then warmed me from the inside out.

"I want you in my bed tonight. I know during the day we need to be careful around Malachi, and I agree with that. But tonight, once he's asleep. I want you with me. We've only had the one night, but I need to be inside you."

My eyes widened as I noticed the bulge in his swim trunks thickening and lengthening right in front of me. Just the memory of our night together had my core pulsing. We'd been so good these past few weeks, not rushing anything between us, especially if we were going to try to make things work. Holding back and not inviting him into my bed those nights he'd been at the house had been hard as hell. Just because we were trying to do things the right way didn't mean it was easy. I wanted him just as much as he wanted me. "And I want you inside me."

"The days are for Malachi and for the three of us to connect. But your nights are mine."

There was nothing else to say, so I simply nodded.

"Good," he said, standing up. He adjusted his shorts to camouflage the thick bulge. "I'm glad you're here with me. There's no one else I'd want to share this with, other than you." Leaning down, he captured my lips with his. One of his hands came to rest on top of my breast. His fingers rubbed along the soft flesh before grasping my nipple between his thumb and middle finger.

He squeezed.

I whimpered.

He rubbed his palm over the stiffening flesh.

My channel slickened as my body prepared itself for more.

Hunter pulled back, removing both his lips and his hand from my body.

I wanted to lunge up and make him do it again. Yeah, I had it bad for this man.

"Later, sweetheart. Right now, I have sandcastles to build with little man."

I couldn't help the smirk that came over my face. Lifting one hand, I pointed at his shorts. "You may want to do something about that before you head down to the beach. I wouldn't want anyone to have the wrong impression."

He didn't even glance down before responding. "I'll think of the last financial reports I reviewed for the company. That'll take care of it." He turned away and began walking away from me, heading back toward Sarah and Malachi.

It was happening too fast. My feelings for Hunter were becoming too much. But he was too damn good to me, and I was falling under his spell. I just hoped I wouldn't be left shattered and heartbroken once it was all over.

Twelve
Anya

Closing the door to Malachi's temporary room at the vacation house, I pressed my forehead to the wooden barrier. Today had been magical. For the first time, Malachi had experienced the beach and playing in the sand, building castles. My little boy's laughter was on repeat all day. His squeals of unfiltered joy made my heart swell. Being a single mother wasn't what I'd planned for my life, but this is who I was. For three years, it had always been me and my beautiful little boy. But today gave me a glimpse into a life that could be. I saw the world through my son's eyes, and I knew what he was missing.

There was only so much I could do for him. Not that I felt we were lacking. But I know there was something to be said about living life freely, without a care in the world. Closing my eyes, I tried to rein in my thoughts. It felt like I was all over the place. One second, I wanted Hunter to stop using his power and influence to do things for me. On the other hand, it felt nice to be pampered for once in my life. To have my every need taken care of.

"Is he asleep?" Hunter asked, walking up behind me as I stood at the door.

His large frame was flush with mine, his chest pressing against my back. I could feel the warmth of his body, even though he wasn't touching me. I'd been craving his touch these past two weeks, but holding off had been a source of pride. At least it was for me.

It felt like I was proving something to myself. That I could resist him. That sex wasn't the only reason I wanted to be with him. Foolish? Probably. But that was now out the window because this weekend would change everything. I just hoped I was ready for what was about to happen.

Turning around, I looked at Hunter standing in front of me. "Yes. Finally. He was so excited about all the things he did today. It took two stories before he closed his eyes. Thank you for this."

"You're welcome," he responded with a smile. "I'm glad you agreed to come away with me."

As I looked at him, I couldn't help but admire the man standing in front of me. A pair of workout shorts sat low on his hips and his chest was bare. The smattering of dark blond hair on his chest, his sculpted abs, the Adonis belt visible just above the waistband of his shorts. As my gaze traveled the length of his body, I knew there was no escaping, not that I wanted to. I wanted to press against him and take what he so freely offered.

"Like what you see?" He asked, stepping closer to me.

Tilting my head up, I nodded. "I do."

He took a deep breath before lifting one hand to cup my face. "Having you here with me is exactly what I needed."

"Why?" I needed to know if he felt the same way I did. If I were in this alone, I could deal with it. It would hurt like hell, but I could control myself and my feelings. Take this for what it was and move on.

"I've missed being with you. These past two weeks have been hard as hell. Literally," he laughed.

Don't say it, Anya. Don't ruin the moment.

"What happens after this weekend?" *I can't believe I asked that question. What is wrong with me? Was I trying to sabotage this?*

He smiled. I melted.

"Nothing changes. We see where this goes. I spend time with you and Malachi. You and I continue to focus on making each other feel good." Leaning his head down, he captured my lips in a kiss. His tongue rolling along my lips as he coaxed me to open for him. Hell, I was ready to do just about anything he asked of me. Deepening the kiss, he used the hand at my waist to pull me closer.

I heard myself whimper in supplication. Losing myself in his kiss, I pressed my body against his. The feel of his member thickening caused my body to respond. My channel slickened in response as I basked in his touch. His kisses. His moans. I could feel myself falling under his spell, and I was happy to go where he wanted. Hunter broke the kiss, nibbling on my lips, before placing soft kisses on my neck, my shoulder, and back to my lips.

Did you hear that? Yeah, the sigh that escaped my mouth was unmistakably filled with lust and need.

I figured it was time to stop fighting how I felt about him.

"Sarah knows to be ready just in case Malachi wakes up," he whispered in my ear.

"You've taken care of everything," I sighed in return, stepping closer.

He nodded. "I wanted this weekend to be perfect for us."

My hands trailed up and down his broad back, which made me realize I was still in the cradle of his arms as well. I moved to step back so I could look at him, but his hold on me tightened.

"I made you a promise earlier, and I mean to fulfill it. Tonight, you're mine." Swooping down, he picked me up, cradling me in his arms as he walked out of my suite and across the hallway.

It wasn't a long walk, but it felt like a shift in the air happened. I wasn't prepared for the feeling that came over me. Reaching my hand up, I caressed his jaw. When he looked down at me after stepping into his room, he smiled. Using his foot, he pushed the door shut with a definite click.

"You're good at this," I couldn't help but respond. My mind immediately questioned how many women he'd carried into this room, or rooms like this one. The excitement coursing through me quickly turned to jealousy, even though I probably had no right to feel this way. As if he could read my thoughts, he shook his head as he adjusted my body, laying me on the king-sized bed sitting in the middle of the room.

He stood over me, his hands resting on his lean hips. "You're thinking too loud, Anya. I'm here with you. Only you. What happened before we met has no bearing on what's happening between us right now."

Ashamed that he could tell what I was thinking so clearly, I averted my gaze. We'd only known each other for three weeks, and one of those weeks we didn't speak or see each other. My feelings for him were unreasonable. Right?

"Look at me," he demanded.

Briefly closing my eyes, I turned my head in his direction as he requested. His intense gaze seared me to the spot. From his look, I could feel the heat course through me.

"I'm here with you. I've been here with you. Stop questioning what's happening between us," Hunter said in a low voice. Goosebumps raised along my skin. He ran a hand down my arm before reaching my bare thigh. I was still wearing a short summer dress that I'd changed into after our afternoon at the beach. "Can you give me what I need, Anya?"

His question was straightforward, but it felt like I agreed to something I wasn't fully aware of. But there was no other answer I could give... "Yes."

A wicked smile came over his face. "If you like that dress, you'd better take it off. My patience is thin. I've been waiting too long for this moment and I'm on edge."

As he spoke, I slid the dress from my shoulders. I wasn't a small woman, but the dress had a built-in bra. My hands shook as I slide the soft material over my body. His eyes never left my body. I could see the color of his eyes darken the longer he looked at me. Shivers coursed through me, and the desire I felt for him increased with every passing second. Once my breasts were free, he raised one hand to run his fingers along my flesh.

"You're so fucking beautiful," his voice was raw, needy.

My mouth moved, trying to form words to respond, but nothing came out. I could feel my channel clenching in time with his every touch. As my breathing sped up, my chest rose and fell, as if trying to push closer to him. My dress pooled around my waist as I lay prone in front of him. I felt open. Raw. Scared of the way I felt about him.

Hunter shifted his gaze as he took in my form. He took a few steps closer to me. Once he was within arm's length, he trailed his hand down my calf. "Do you know, the first time I saw you, I was struck dumb. When you walked into the bar at the tower, I knew you were meant for me."

A laugh escaped. "But aren't you the consummate bachelor? I've seen the pictures of you with all the different women. Why would I be the one for you?" At my comment, he lifted his gaze to mine. The snap of frustration was clear for me to see.

"Didn't we have the conversation already?" Placing his hands on my hips, he pushed the material of my dress further down my body. "Lift." Once my hips were off the bed, he removed the dress, pulling it down my body before throwing it over his shoulder.

There I lay, in only a pair of panties. If he looked close enough, I'm positive he'd be able to see the wetness seeping from between my legs. I wanted to feel embarrassed, but I knew it was no use. I'd made a commitment to no longer hide my feelings from Hunter. That started today. Right now. In this super-sized bedroom with the King-sized bed.

"Sweetheart, you're here with me, yet you keep bringing up the past," he sounded exasperated. "Have you seen me with anyone since I met you?"

I shook my head. "No," and believe me, I'd looked.

"Because from the moment you walked into my life, I knew things were going to change," he said, his hand traveling back up from my leg to my thigh, to my panty-covered mound.

A moan sounded in the room and I knew it was from me. Hunter's thumb made lazy circles on the hardened flesh between my legs. The feeling was so intense, I moved to raise my hips, silently begging him for more. I whimpered in need.

"No, baby. This is my show. I need you to lie back and enjoy."

Lay here and enjoy? Was he crazy? "You know that's not happening, Hunter."

"As I was saying. Meeting you that night helped me see things clearly. I'm not a perfect man...."

"But you're pretty damn close."

Shaking his head, he rubbed his hand along my curved stomach. Tempted to suck it in and pull away, I forced myself to stay where I was. To let him explore me the way he wanted, without interruption.

"No, I'm far from perfect. Hopefully, you'll never have to experience that, and all you'll see is the man in front of you right now. For you, and Malachi, I'm going to be about as perfect as I can be. I just need you to have patience. This is new for me."

Although I wasn't sure what he was referring to, I would not deny him. "I'm not going anywhere." And I meant every word.

Walking to the end of the bed, Hunter grabbed at my panties and pulled them down my body.

"Damn, baby. You're so fucking wet and we haven't even started. Is all that for me?" He pulled the slip of material from my body before spreading my legs. Climbing on top of the soft mattress, he glared up at me. "Don't take your eyes off me. Not for one second. Do you hear me?" he growled.

Nodding in response, I could feel my body vibrate with anticipation.

"Use your words, Anya."

"Yes. I hear you." I gasped at the feel of his tongue against my bare slit. Oh, damn.

Thirteen
Anya

My body felt out of control. Charged with energy. The only thing that kept the feeling from being overwhelming was grabbing hold of Hunter's strong shoulders and tightening my hands on his flesh. My fingers grabbed his skin, nails digging deep as his tongue swiped against my bare mound. Hunter covered my entire slit with his mouth before sliding his tongue along my quivering flesh. The moan that came from my mouth was unlike any sound I'd made before. His hands grasped my thighs, pushing them back, my knees almost to my shoulders.

As he focused on my most sensitive area, his tongue met my clit. With a growl, he sucked the swollen nubbin into his mouth and sucked. Hard.

A keening wail rent the air as my orgasm soared through my body. My hands fought for purchase, gripping the strands of his hair. My body shook as Hunter feasted on me. The sounds of his mouth licking and sucking at me as my juices flowed ratcheted up my body's reaction, creating even more amazing sensations. My cries and moans and whimpers filled the room as his mouth devoured me. Toes curling, hips lifting. I wanted more. Needed more. And then he gave me exactly what I was hoping for.

Hunter shifted one hand from my thigh, tracing a pattern along my leg until he came to my pulsating mound. Gathering some of my juices on his finger, he pushed it deep inside me. A loud "Oomph" escaped as the pressure of his finger penetrating my body collided with the tightening of my sheath as I orgasmed.

Hunter lifted his head for a second. "Tastiest fucking treat I've had in a while. Now, give me what I need. Open up, sweetheart." Even as he spoke, he continued to thrust his digit inside me, then adding a second one to the mix. It was almost too much, but at the same time, I needed him to never stop.

"Please, Hunter. Don't stop." My gaze was still on him. I dared not look away from him. I knew he was preparing me for the grand finale when he slid his thick member inside my body. Tears leaked from my eyes as I anticipated how tonight would end.

"Never," he said before dipping his head again and latching onto me.

My body trembled. I cursed him. I pleaded with him. I thanked whatever deity was listening for bringing Hunter into my life. His hair was still within my grasp as I pulled and twisted. I wanted my cream all over his face. I wanted him to never forget just how good I tasted. If I had my wish, I'd keep him so satisfied this weekend, he could never walk away from me.

His tight grasp on my thigh was the only thing keeping me from squirming off the bed. My body was filled with ecstasy. How could it feel this damn good? He was overwhelming my senses. I was ruined for anyone else. I couldn't imagine any other man doing to me what Hunter could. It just wasn't possible. Hunter pulled my clit between his mouth, grasping the hardened flesh within his teeth, lightly clamping down. Lightning flashed behind my eyes, and my mouth opened in a wail. Hunter shifted his body, one hand covering my mouth as he continued to thrust his fingers inside of me, and his mouth suckled my flesh. My back arched as my body seized in pleasure.

In my mind, I was pleading with him to continue. To stop. To go even harder. Then I begged for more. Although none of the words escaped my mouth, it was as if he heard everything I said. After a few moments of feeling like I was suspended in the air, I collapsed back on the bed. I began pushing Hunter away. I needed to escape. It was too much. If he continued, I wouldn't be able to control myself.

Hunter leaned back, removing his hand from my mouth and his fingers from my body. He ran his tongue over his lips as if savoring the flavor he had found there. "Fuck, you taste good."

"I need you inside me," I whispered. My arms reaching out for him.

"As you wish," he said in a gravelly tone.

Grabbing my legs again, he pulled my body closer to him. I noticed he was fully naked. Although I didn't see when he stripped out of his shorts, I was sure that I was too far gone to pay attention to anything but how he'd made me feel. In one swift motion, my body was flush against his. His rock-hard cock was hot and pressing against my body.

"Yes," I hissed. My legs widened in anticipation.

Leaning over, he trailed one hand down my face, his thumb rubbing along my bottom lip. "You belong to me, Anya."

My natural retort would be to deny his claim. I belonged to no man. But as I looked into his blue eyes and waited for the moment when he'd join our bodies together, it was time for me to rethink that response. I belonged to him. There was no shame in that. But did he belong to me?

Pushing that thought out of my head, I reached down to take hold of him. Wrapping my hand around the velvet steel pressing against my body, I moaned in surrender. All my doubts about us, and what I meant to him, disappeared. I'd worry about the 'what if' questions tomorrow. Tonight, I only wanted to focus on this right here. How he made me feel. The look on his face as he stared down at my naked form.

"Give it to me, Hunter," I plead.

I pull him closer to me, pressing him inside my body. This was the best way I could think of to let him know I was ready for him. That I was tired of waiting.

"Stop," he growled. Instinctively, I did. Lifting my eyes to his, I noticed the blaze of desire as he stared down at me. He removes my hand from his thick member and grabs both my arms, placing them above my head. One hand clasps my wrist together, while the other guided him toward my slick channel.

"You want me inside you, Anya? You want me to slide inside you and claim you as mine? I know those thoughts in your head right now are battling for supremacy. Tell me you want me to fuck you, baby."

"Yeah…" I whispered into the silence.

He shook his head. "No. Say the words."

"Fuck me, Hunter. I want it. I want you," I moan as he grabs my hands, lifting them over my head. The next sensation I feel is him sliding inside my slick channel. "Oh, God."

"God ain't got shit to do with this. Say my name."

Say his name? I can't even remember my own damn name. All I can focus on is the feel of him as he slides inside me. Stretching me in ways I hadn't known before him, and I doubted I would feel once we went our separate ways.

He surged inside me. "Say my fucking name, Anya," his voice demanded me to respond.

"Hunter," I gasped. "Hunter." I'd say that shit on repeat as long as he never stopped. As he began stroking deeply inside my body, I almost stop breathing at the feeling coursing through me. "Yes," I moan.

He continues to pump inside me with a smooth, deep rhythm. Slow and steady at first, teasing with me with his sensual strokes. Then he speeds up, moving faster and faster, building up the tension. I clench around him. My nails dig into my palms as he continues to hold both my hands above my head. "Let me touch you."

"No. Not yet. This is my time. I want to see that look on your face as I fuck you. I want you to recognize just how much I need to be inside you. How much I need you."

I can't hold on. The sensation is too much. The feeling is overwhelming. I'm spiraling. My eyes rolled to the back of my head. As my legs wrap around his waist, I match his rhythm as he goes harder, deeper. I want all he has. Everything that he wants to give. My hands itch to touch him, to hold on to him as I fall over the cliff. "Please," I beg.

He doesn't stop. His rhythm stays smooth as he thrusts inside me. His lips are against my neck, placing soft kisses along my skin. "Please what, Anya?"

My mind goes blank for a second. What was I asking him? Because the only thing on my mind right now is how good this feels. Every push and pull takes me to the precipice, and I want to fall over. My eyes roll back in my head when he goes deep and stays there.

"Do you know how fucking good you feel? I can't get enough of you."

"I want to touch you," I finally manage to get the words out. "Please, let me touch you."

At first, I don't think he's going to answer. He leans down to kiss me on the lips. I can feel another orgasm coming. I want to cry and whimper and beg him to give me more. The words trapped in my mind want to plead with him to never let me go. Even in this blissful state, I hold back. It's one thing to think the words. It's something different to put those words out in the air.

Suddenly, Hunter releases my hands. Adjusting his position, he grabs my hair with one hand, the other holds my chin. "You drive me so goddamned crazy." He nipped at my chin, my lips, just before swiping his tongue over the spot he'd just abused.

"I know," I whisper, grabbing him around his waist.

The twist of his fingers in my hair caused a surge of pain and pleasure to ripple within my body. My scalp feels the pain, but my body feels the pleasure. How is this possible? The top of his pelvis rubs against the bundle of nerves at the apex of my thighs.

"I'm not letting you go."

"No one asked you to," I sass back at him.

Leaning down, he captures my lips in a kiss, his tongue mimicking the motions of his cock as he surged inside me. His body shifted upward, creating a new type of friction. I broke away from the kiss because I needed to breathe. It was too much.

"Oh, fuck. Hunter," I moan in pleasure.

"Give it all to me, baby. I want every moan, every word. This is only for me," he says to me as his body speeds up. "Come for me, Anya."

I want nothing more. The quiver that courses through me is in direct response to his command. The clenching of my channel around his thick member tells me that even if I wanted to hold back, it wasn't possible.

"Stop holding back," he demands. "Give it to me. It's mine, and I want what's mine," he barks at me.

I detonate around him. My body surges up, my mouth falls open in a silent scream, and my nails scrape against his bare skin. Yet, he doesn't stop. He continues to stroke. Push. Pull. Thrust.

Even as my body clenches around him, he continued to stroke and drive me out of my mind. Words have no meaning for me right now, so I don't even try. Mumbles and gibberish are the only sounds escaping my mouth, but I'm quite sure Hunter knows that's a good thing.

"That's what the fuck I'm talking about. Give it to me, Anya. I want it all." Hunter's thrusts become erratic, but at this point, I'm just along for the ride. I'm like a rag doll, here for all the pleasure I can take without passing out. "Yes. Yes," he repeatedly says, until he freezes above me, his body surging one last time. I can feel him pulse as he releases. Once he finishes, he places one last kiss on my lips before moving to the side, pulling himself out of my body. "I'm so glad I met you."

I nod in response, but my eyes remain closed. "Me too." Hunter wraps his arms around me, pulling me closer. Unwelcome tears fill my eyes because I know I've fallen for a man who's made no promises or commitments for the future. I'm not sure how I got in this situation, but now that I'm here, I need to figure out how the hell I'm going to handle it.

Fourteen
Hunter

Sitting on the deck the next morning, I tried focusing on the scene in front of me. The view was amazing, the waves crashing against the shore, the smell of the ocean, and peace. No matter how much I tried to keep my mind clear, I couldn't stop thinking about the woman inside the house behind me, the one lying in bed where I'd left her this morning. When my eyes opened this morning, my first thought was that I wanted to take her again. I was hard as hell. Memories of last night flowed through my mind in quick succession. Just thinking about sliding inside Anya's body made me thicken in my shorts. The sounds of her moans and sighs of pleasure rang in my ears, bringing a smile to my face. I wanted nothing more than to hear those sounds from her again.

After that first time, I took her two more times. We didn't fall asleep until well after two in the morning. She needed her rest. I'd be an asshole to wake her just because I wanted to slake my lust. Rubbing one hand over my burgeoning length, I tried to think of something else. Anything else to prevent me from going inside and doing what I wanted to her. I needed to give her at least a few more hours.

Taking a drink of my coffee, I glanced down at my phone and noticed a few missed calls from Stewart, my chief financial officer. I knew exactly why he was calling, but he could wait. If he and Dan couldn't handle one day without me being around, then what the fuck was I paying them for? I told them I wanted one fucking day and yet there were four calls between them. Was it a wise decision not to call them back? Probably not. I knew, and so did they, that if something went wrong with this deal, they would both be out of a job before I could snap my fingers. There were two things people shouldn't fuck with. My money and my business.

Glancing out at the water again, a vision of how Anya looked this morning, lying naked on the white sheets. Her brown skin was a deep contrast, trying to draw me back into the bed with her. Okay, make that four things people shouldn't fuck with, because Anya and Malachi were now included on that list.

Sighing, I stood and walked over to the railing of the wraparound porch. From the outside looking in, I was the epitome of calm. I was a swirling tornado of emotions on the inside, and I didn't like it one bit. When did she come to mean so much to me? Was I ready for what it meant to be with Anya? She was a single mother used to surviving on her own. As my woman, the life she had today was not how it would be for her tomorrow. Inevitably, things would change. Being with me could provide her with a life and open doors for her she hadn't expected. The question was, would she accept that from me?

Smiling, I lifted my cup of coffee to my lips, taking a sip of the tepid liquid. She wouldn't really have a choice. I was an all-or-nothing type of man. Anya would come to know that soon enough.

My phone rang again. When I looked down at the screen, I noticed it was Dan. Again.

Sighing, I answered. "What?"

"Where have you been? I've been calling you all morning."

I pulled the phone away from my ear and looked at the screen. This motherfucker did not just come at me like this. Placing the phone against my ear again, my voice cut through his ramblings. "Dan, I'm not sure what the fuck you're thinking, but don't ever fucking call me again and speak to me with that tone in your voice. You forget yourself, but I will give you a lesson so that you remember. Understood?" At his silence, I repeated myself, much louder. "Am I understood?"

"Uh-uh, yes, Mr. Malone. I understand," he stammered on the other side of the phone.

I took a deep breath. "Now, what the fuck are you calling me for this early? I told you I needed the day. Are you not capable of handling shit when I'm not there? Between you and Stewart, there's half-a-million in salary." Silence. "What is the issue, Dan?"

"Fuck," he whispered.

"Realizing this call should never have happened?" I taunted.

He began to speak, and I tried to calm down. I didn't want my day or weekend with

Anya and Malachi ruined by work. As the company owner, taking time off wasn't something I regularly did, but when I did take a break from the office, I expected my time off to be respected. This phone call was not respecting my time.

"They raised the asking price for the software. And instead of allowing us to acquire it outright, they want us to purchase licenses. They're balking. They want to keep ownership of the software but force us to pay them an annual fee to use it." Dan paused. I could hear him exhale from the other side of the line. "They're threatening to walk away if we don't agree to their terms."

"Fuck," I yelled out, throwing my coffee mug against the wall. "How did this happen? When I last spoke with them earlier this week, there were no hints of an issue. They were on board with the deal as presented." Pacing along the wooden deck, I ran my fingers through my hair. If this deal fell through, it would set us back another six months. That's not something I was willing to do. "We need to find out what changed."

"Yes, that's why we've been calling. I know you're away for the weekend, but Stewart and I want to know how far we can push on this. They're asking for an answer by Monday morning. Which gives us three days to decide."

I listened silently, thoughts swirling in my head. While I wasn't happy about having my weekend interrupted, I knew Dan was right to reach out to me. The deal had been in play for over six months. For them to throw a wrench into the plan this late meant something else had happened. "Someone else is going after them. They're playing us against each other." Was I willing to destroy a small company to get what I wanted? Fuck yes, I was. They'd learn not to fuck around with my business and my money. This was a lesson they'd never forget.

"Put the word out that we're pulling out of the deal. That the software has a flaw and that we're going in another direction."

"Is that really what we're doing? Pulling out of the deal?" Dan asked. I could hear the frustration in his voice, but I didn't give a shit.

I hadn't been the only one focused on this deal for the past six months. My entire team knew just how much this could change things for us. That didn't mean I enjoyed being questioned.

"Do what I asked you to do. If they reach out to you about it, ignore their calls. I want this to go right to the wire on Monday. I want to raise doubt in their product and bring them to the brink."

Dan sighed. "I know we want to play hardball, but what if there's no other company involved? What if they're just trying to stay viable and keep ownership of the product they created?"

"They should have thought of that before changing the parameters of the deal when we're ready to sign-off. Let them pay the price for their stupidity. If they don't sell to us, it won't matter what they wanted because I'll shut them the fuck down. Now, do what the fuck I said. They'll either come running to us on Monday ready to sign the original terms, or their company will go down in flames. It's their choice."

"You got it."

"And don't bother me again until Monday morning."

"Hunter—"

I swiped the screen to end the call. There was nothing more to be said. Yes, I understood why they were calling, but it also pissed me off that I had to deal with it today. On any given day, I would happily focus on my business, but fuck, I just needed three fucking days to myself. Was that so damn hard?

Realizing I had nothing to drink because I'd thrown my coffee against the side of the house, I turned to walk over to the tables on the side of the deck that held hot and cold food, plus coffee and juice. As soon as I faced the table, I noticed Anya standing there staring at me. She wore a yellow sundress that reached down to her knees. Her hair was pulled back and twisted on top of her head. There was no make-up on her face, but then again, she didn't need it. I'm sure she thought wearing that shit on her face made her look better, but I never thought she needed it. Anya was beautiful just the way she was, and she was all mine. "Morning, baby," I greeted her.

She looked away from me. What the fuck was that all about? I walked over to stand in front of her. Using one hand, I placed it under her chin before tilting her head. After the night we had, I wanted to look into her eyes. "Good morning, Anya."

"Good morning, Hunter," she whispered, sliding her gaze away from me again.

Leaning down, I kissed her softly on her lips. "How are you feeling?"

Her gaze fell for a second as her hands fidgeted. "A little sore."

I couldn't help the smile that came over my face. Pressing closer, I wrapped one arm around Anya's waist, pulling her body close to mine. "Good. I want you to remember last night and every night we're together. Just know, I'm gonna wear your ass out again tonight, so you might want to do some stretches or soak in a bath or some shit." Her laughter at my comments made me smile. Staring down at her, I knew she still had to be tired. "I thought you'd still be sleeping."

She ran her hands down my chest. "I was, but Malachi was up and running around, so I got up as well."

I nodded. "Did he see you come out of my bedroom?" That was one of her concerns about being here with me. Anya was worried that Malachi would see something that would confuse him. Hell, I was ready to shout it from the rooftops. On the other hand, Anya was still hesitant to share our relationship with the world. For some reason, that bothered the hell out of me, but I'd tackle that situation later. *One issue at a time, Hunter.*

"No, thank goodness." She leaned up on her toes and pressed her lips against mine before pulling back. "He was too busy playing hide and seek with Sarah to pay attention to his mom. But once he saw me, he made it known that he was ready to eat."

"Where is he now?" Lifting my gaze, I looked through the window to see him sitting at a table in the kitchen eating what looked like waffles.

"Stuffing his face. When we came down, you were on the phone. It looked... intense. I thought it was best to keep inside for a few minutes while I came outside." Her brown gaze caught mine, and I could see the nervousness in her eyes. "Is everything okay?"

I smiled. "Of course, everything's fine. Just a bit of business that had to be handled." Anya separated her body from mine, and I immediately missed her warmth. "We shouldn't be interrupted again." We'd better not be interrupted, or else someone would lose their damn job.

"If having us here is a distraction or you need to handle business, I don't mind if you take us home."

"Stop that," I growled. "You and Malachi are the best kind of distraction. You're here with me because I want you to be. Nothing takes priority over the two of you this weekend."

"If you say so," she said before walking over to the food-laden table.

From her tone, I know she didn't fully believe me. "I'll just have to make sure I prove that to you," I said in response. At that moment, I took things in a different direction. "Once you and Malachi finish eating, I have plans for us."

Fifteen
Hunter

I was in my bedroom waiting for Anya to show up. Our day together had been perfect, or at least my idea of perfection. Spending time with her and Malachi opened my eyes. Allowed me to see the world through the eyes of a three-year-old little boy. Of course, intellectually, I know I was his age before. At one point, I was full of innocence and saw the joy in everything around me. That feeling left me years ago after watching my mother have her spirit crushed under my father's thumb for so many years.

The happiness on Malachi's face as we built sandcastles on the beach wasn't something I would ever forget. The look on his face when the chef brought out the dessert piled high with chocolate, caramel, and marshmallows brought a smile to my face. If I could have captured that moment in time with a photo, I would have.

As I was thinking about all the fun we had earlier that day with Malachi, my bedroom door opened and Anya stepped inside. My thoughts shifted to her, and only her.

This woman had no idea what she did to me. How she made me want something more. After seeing how my mother was treated by my father, the whole marriage, kids, white picket fence, and Sunday dinners at the table had never been a dream for me. I ran away from commitment as fast as I could. Commitment and marriage trapped you into a false sense of security. But money, ah money, that could change your life.

No more wearing second-hand clothes. No more asking the state for assistance to buy groceries for your family. No more seeing the looks of disdain and disgust in the eyes of your neighbors.

That was the future I envisioned for myself, and I made it happen. My brother, Caleb, felt the same way. We didn't blame our mother for staying—well, maybe we did a little—but as kids, all we cared about was being with her. Our only focus was being there with her whenever our dad came home drunk, angry at the world for the perceived slights against him. I promised myself and Caleb that I'd do whatever it takes to get us the hell outta there and never look back.

I focused on getting good grades in school. I ignored the taunts of the kids who didn't understand that I had no choice but to wear the clothes they'd deemed unworthy and had given away to the thrift store. From the time I was ten, everything I did was focused on becoming better, smarter, stronger than anyone else around me. When I was fifteen, I found football. That one shift changed my life.

It's a funny thing about playing football and being good at it. All the flaws others once saw in you seem to disappear. All the taunts once lobbed at you by the popular kids become pats on the back and invites to the best parties. Life changed for me, and it happened without me even noticing. At least, not until I walked into a classroom one day and everyone vied for my attention instead of turned away.

Some people would say I became harder, colder, more ruthless in my ambition. My focus on being the best was all there was. It was the only thing that mattered. As for me, I think that was when I became the real Hunter. It was a prelude to the man standing here today. With my first name being Hunter, it was easy to picture everyone else as the prey. It's just how life was for me back then, and it was who I am today. And I was happy with the man I was. Women flocked to me like bees on honey. All I had to do was make a phone call and things fell in my lap. I wanted for nothing. Until this moment.

"Hi," Anya said in a tone laced with desire.

At this moment, everything else faded to the background. I wanted Anya with a fierceness that surprised me. All the other women meant nothing to me. Having her in my arms, underneath me, with those beautiful eyes looking at me as I slid inside her, was the only thing I needed right now.

"Hey, baby. Come here," I beckoned her from the other side of the room. I stood at the French doors leading out to a balcony. The sound of the ocean waves crashing against the shore serenaded us.

Once Anya stood in front of me, I grabbed her around the waist. "I've been waiting for you," I whispered.

"Malachi took longer to get to sleep. He wouldn't stop talking about the sandcastles and dessert, which was too much, by the way. And the dune buggy ride. How did you manage that?"

Lifting one eyebrow, I looked down at her. "Really? How did I arrange a simple thing like a dune buggy ride? You know me better than that by now."

She laughed, nodding her head. "Okay, that's true. You seem to have the magic touch. You snap your fingers, and people seem to jump to do your bidding."

I smiled, then snapped my fingers.

"Why'd you just snap—"

"I'm testing out your theory. If I snap my fingers, will you do my bidding?"

Wrapping her arms around my neck, she played with the strands in my hair. "Aren't I already doing your bidding? This weekend, I dropped everything to get you. I come to you at night so you can do what you want to my body. I think it's safe to say that I'm addicted to you."

My head dipped down, capturing her lips in a deep kiss. She may not realize it, but she was my drug of choice. Moving one hand, I gathered the hem of her sundress and skimmed my bare hand along her thigh. Just the feel of her skin took me to another place. I could feel myself hardening within my pants as we stood under the moonlight giving ourselves to each other. Being with Anya made me feel alive in a way I never expected. Not sure how I'd been so lucky to have her walk into my life, but there was no way in hell I was ever letting her go. I broke the kiss before staring down into her face.

Her eyes were half-closed, and she looked dazed. A surge of pride coursed through me. Knowing that it was me who made her feel this way caused my lips to lift in a smile. Bending slightly, I lifted her in my arms. Anya wrapped her arms around my neck.

"You're gonna get enough of lifting me. I'm not light, you know," she groused.

Walking over to the bed, I held her in my arms for a while longer. "You weigh nothing. Stop saying shit that pisses me off, Anya. If I want to lift you and walk around this whole fucking house, I will."

A huge smile came over her face, and she kissed me softly. "You know how to make a woman feel good."

Shaking my head, I shifted so I could lay her down on the bed. "I'm not trying to make any other woman feel good. I'm only focused on you, Anya. If you feel good, that's all I care about." I know my behavior from the past two weeks made her question if I was serious about her. I know it was stupid, but I was also testing myself as well.

Could I be with someone for more than one night?

Was I capable of putting all the other women aside to focus my attention on one woman?

The answers to those questions had been a resounding yes.

I know it hadn't been fair to Anya, but I had to go through the process my own way. Hell, I'd even talked to my friend Conall about it. He had a different take, of course. Now, let's be honest, I know precisely who Conall is and what he's capable of. When he told me he met his wife through his alternate world, I knew some shit must have gone down. But the thing he stressed to me was that at some point, I'd have to decide.

The day would come when I'd have to go all-in or let her walk away. I'd struggled with that question for days.

Was being with Anya more important than all the other bullshit?

Did the thought of not being with her make the world a little darker, harsher, and colder?

Conall and Tatiana's story was not mine to tell, but I know they went through some serious shit to be together. If they could make it through, then I know me and Anya and Malachi could do the same.

"Hunter?" Anya called out to me. "Where'd you go just now? Everything okay?"

Coming back to the present moment, I nodded. "Yeah, baby. Everything's perfect." Quickly stripping off my clothes, I stood naked in front of her within moments. When she reached up her hands to remove her dress, I stopped her. "No. Let me."

As her body was unveiled to me inch-by-inch, I couldn't help but appreciate the way she was formed. Her beautiful mahogany skin, smooth and soft all over. Plump lips that kissed me so softly. Her full breasts weren't small, but they fit perfectly in the palm of my hands. The trail of stretch marks on her stomach that bore testament to the gift of life she'd given Malachi. Her thick thighs that cradled me so beautifully every time I found my home inside her.

Anya's hands came up to cover the parts of her body I was focused on appreciating. "Don't hide from me."

"Hunter," she sighed. "I'm not perfect. When you look at me that way, I want to turn away. Hide the flaws that I don't want you to see."

My eyes snapped to her face. "I said don't hide from me." Her hands shifted quickly, moving back to the mattress. "You are beautiful. Every inch of you is perfect. I know what you look like, sweetheart. Have you forgotten how many times I've kissed the soft skin of your stomach, trailed my hands over your body, or stared at your naked form after we've fucked? Did you know, our first night together, I watched you sleep?"

She shook her head. "No. Why'd you do that? I was probably drooling. Staring at me while I looked all crazy and junk. What's wrong with you? Crazy man."

"Don't talk like that. Even then, I knew you were something special to me. You were so free. So open. Every time you moaned my name, I committed it to memory. There was something about the way your voice whispered for me to give you more that made me want to give you everything."

Anya smiled, lifting one hand to brush along my thigh.

I smiled down at her. "We couldn't get enough of each other. I didn't want to take my eyes off you." I pinched one nipple between my two fingers. "Do you know what I realized?"

She shook her head, her eyes never leaving my face. "No," she whispered.

"I couldn't take my eyes off you because I was afraid you'd disappear. When the sun came up, I watched you. I memorized every inch of your body. I felt that if I went to sleep, you wouldn't be there when I opened my eyes. Then when I couldn't help it any longer, I closed my eyes."

My fingers teased her mouth, pressing and pulling at the sensitive skin of her mound.

"Can you guess what happened when I woke up? When I looked over at the other side of the bed, expecting to find you there?"

When she stayed silent, biting her bottom lip as my touch became more insistent. I should let it go, but I wanted an answer. Something inside me needed her to acknowledge what she'd done. Grabbing her clit between my thumb and forefinger, I pinched and tugged on her bundle of nerves. Not hard, but with just enough pressure to make sure she felt that bite of pain. Her moans of pleasure sounded loud in the room. Her legs opened wider as I manipulated her soft flesh.

"Fuck, Hunter."

"Tell me what happened when I opened my eyes, Anya," I demanded.

"I was gone," she gasped. "You were alone."

Releasing her clit, I rubbed against the wet flesh before taking one finger and pressing inside her pulsing channel. "You left me alone, just as I thought you might. But now that I have you again, I'm not going to let you go," I growled, plunging my digit inside her body. Adding a second finger, I watched her unravel from my touch. My thumb pressed against the hardened flesh peeking out at me from her labia. Fuck, I needed to taste her. But before I did that, I wanted to see her lose control.

"Hunter," she whimpered. "Please."

"Please what?" I said, my fingers continuing to bring her over the edge.

"More. Please, more," Anya pleaded.

"Anything for you." And to my surprise, I meant every fucking word.

Curling my fingers inside her, I hit that special place that I'd been seeking. Her body seized up, a keening wail released from her throat, and her channel pulsed, squeezing my digits as her orgasm rushed through her. Leaning down, I brought my face to hers, licking her soft lips as I continued my ministrations. Before this weekend was over, Anya would know who she belonged to.

No one ever called me a nice man. I was ruthless, both in business and in life. She was mine, and I was never letting her go. "I want all of you, baby," and I would accept nothing less.

Sixteen
Hunter

Anya broke apart under my touch. I watched with fascination as sweat droplets raised along her skin. I wanted to swipe at the droplets with my tongue. There was nothing about her that was too much for me. There was only the two of us at this moment. Every moan, whimper, gasp, and clench of her channel was mine for the taking.

Removing my fingers from her, I shifted my body, positioning myself between her legs. I needed to taste her. Wrapping my arms around her upper thighs and hips, I placed my mouth over her, my tongue swiping at the dripping essence. "Fuck," I moaned. So. Fucking. Good.

"Hunter," she squeaked, her hands reaching for me and grabbing strands of my hair. I didn't know if she was pulling me closer or pushing me away. Since I was a man of action, I decided for her. Tightening my grip on her, I pressed my face closer, grabbing her clit with my lips, swirling my tongue against the bundle of nerves. Anya lifted her hips, pushing her mound against me. Yeah, my baby wanted more. Needed more. Just so happens, I was the right man to give her exactly what she was asking for.

My lips and tongue maneuvered around her flesh as if it were the tastiest meal I'd ever had. I nipped, licked, sucked, and slurped around every nook and crevice. Pressing her legs back, I tilted her curvy frame so I could have more access to her body. Anya quivered from head to toe, so I knew what was about to happen. Her moans and gasps filled the room. The sounds escaping her lips were music to my ears. I was so hard and ready to plunge inside her, but I needed this first. The slickness increased. Other than her moans and whimpers, the only other sound was my lips snacking on her as if she were a fucking tasty cake.

"Hunter!" she screamed. Her toes curled. Her hands clawed the bed.

If my face wasn't buried in between her legs, she'd see the wicked smile that came over my face. Just as she went over the edge, I pulled her clit between my lips and began a sucking motion, like drinking through a straw. *Yeah, baby. Give me that gushy stuff.*

I could hear the scream bubbling up to the surface as she broke apart, her body squirming and writhing on the mattress as her body responded to the added stimulation. Quickly adjusting one hand, I placed it over her mouth to cover the sound. Her taste exploded on my tongue and I wanted so much more. I wanted her weeping. I wanted her to look at me and know I was the only man who could do this to her. Me. Hunter Malone. The last man she'd ever be with.

Removing my mouth from her, I pulled myself up and lined up my cock with her pulsing entrance. "Look at me, Anya."

Tears leaked from her eyes. Incoherent moans released from her throat, but she opened her eyes to do as I bid.

"You belong to me, baby. No one else. No other man will have what's mine," I ground out as I notched myself inside her body. The aftershock from her orgasm caused her to clench around the tip of my cock. It took everything inside me not to surge inside her. "Tell me who you belong to," I demanded.

"Y-Y-You. I belong... to you."

"Damned right, you do." My arms rested on the same of her head on the pillow, my hands grabbed at her thick tresses, and I sank inside her, inch my excruciating inch. "You feel so good wrapped around me," I moaned.

"Hunter,"

"Yes, baby. Say my name as I fuck you. You're it for me, Anya. You were made for me," I whispered as I plunged inside her body. My hips pistoned back and forth as we stared into each other's eyes.

"Hunter," she repeated, her legs coming up to wrap around my lean hips.

Shifting my knees, I brought our bodies to an angle, allowing me to go deeper. This wasn't just a fucking; this was a claiming. It felt like I was leaving my mark on her. That any man who saw her from this point forward would know she belonged to me. I'd stomp a hole in any man who tried to take her from me. Pressing deeper, I stroked her just the way I know she liked. And then I heard it… the sound that men fight wars for women since the dawn of time.

"Oooohhhhhh!"

Something snapped in my brain. "That's it, baby. Give me all this pussy. Let Daddy know how much you love me being inside you.

"Hunter," she moaned. "Oooohhhhhh!"

Leaning back, I lifted my upper body. Unwrapping her legs from my waist, I pushed her limbs, pushing them back, her knees practically touching her shoulders. Glancing down, I watched as my glistening member slide inside her. It was a fucking thing of beauty. Every night needed to end like this, with Anya underneath me as I tattooed my name on her body.

Anya whimpered and the sound went straight to my dick. I could fucking swear I swelled even more, becoming even harder as I stroked inside her quivering sheath. If I didn't know better, I'd swear I was in love. But, of course, that wasn't the case. Not yet anyway. Maybe in the future. Right now, all I know is that no other woman had made me feel this good.

Just Anya.

Only Anya.

"Look at me," I growled at her when I realized her eyes had closed. "Watch me. Watch us."

"It's too much," she whimpered.

"No. It's never too much," I countered. Releasing her legs, I pulled her up. "Wrap your legs around my waist." As soon as I felt her do as I asked, I pulled her body up, settling her atop of me. Wrapping my arms around her back, I stared into her eyes. "Never too much. Never enough," I whispered, just before capturing her lips in a kiss. Holding her tight, I lifted her body and pressed her down, allowing her to ride my shaft. We started a slow dance, a rhythm only the two of us knew. Our kiss didn't stop as Anya shuddered on top of me, her entire body jerking and shaking as I felt more of her essence drip down her channel and cover me.

Her head jerked back, breaking the kiss as she ground her pussy on top of me. "You feel so good, Hunter."

"Take all you want," I encouraged.

"Yes," she moaned.

I could see her eyes glaze over as she orgasmed, but the one thing she never did was look away from me. "You're so good to me, Anya."

My body was rebelling at waiting so long. I needed to finish. Anya's hands were in my hair as her head rested at the crook of my neck. Her tongue came out, licking at my skin. I grabbed her closer. I was positive she'd have bruises after tonight. Did I care? No. Because I'd know why she had them. From us being together, from this moment, committing to each other.

I thrust even faster, getting as deep as I could. But it still wasn't deep enough. There was something primal coursing through me, and I needed more. Leaning over, I laid Anya down on the mattress before repositioning her legs over my shoulders. Yes... This is what I needed. The wet sounds of our bodies slapping together was like music to my ears. This was that good shit right here.

"I'm never gonna let you go," I said against her lips.

"Please," she whispered in return.

I knew what she wanted. What she was pleading for. I increased my motions, going deeper each time, the head of my cock kissing her cervix. I wasn't trying to hurt her, but my only thought was claiming her, making her mine.

Tingling started in my toes, traveling up through my legs, thighs, and into my stomach. "Come for me again, baby."

"So good," she whimpered.

"Come for me, Anya."

"Yes. Yes. Yes," she chanted.

Her toes curled as I felt her clamp tight around me. Her sharp nails clawed at my sides as her body shook in release.

I felt my own release coming upon me as I thrust rapidly inside her body. My hips surged forward as my orgasm came over me. "Fuck," I hissed as sensation overtook me. The only thing I knew at this moment was that I was exactly where I belonged.

The very next thought that went through my mind was that I hoped we'd created a life tonight. I may not be capable of falling in love, but that didn't mean Anya wasn't mine. She belonged to me in every sense of the word. If getting her pregnant would solidify that connection, then I'd do whatever it takes to make that happen.

Being a father wasn't something I'd ever considered before now. Still rocking inside her, I tried to prevent my seed from flowing out of her body. I looked down at the woman who already meant so much to me and couldn't help but smile. Getting to know Malachi these past weeks had started something, a feeling of contentment and happiness. Bringing them away with me this weekend was the right decision for me because now I knew what I wanted.

A family of my own.

We'd already talked about medical test results and birth control. The possibility of Anya getting pregnant was about 0.01%, but that didn't mean I couldn't want there to be a miracle.

Bending my head, I kissed her soft lips, our tongues dueling as we both came down from the pinnacle of pleasure. Pulling out of her, I moved to the side before getting up from the bed and walking to the bathroom for a wet cloth. When I stepped back into the room a minute later, I could hear Anya's soft snores. Laughing at the sound, I knew I'd never tell her about it. Women were sensitive about that kind of shit. After wiping her down to remove the sweat and other fluids from her body, I threw the soiled towel in the corner. Grabbing the sheet and blanket, which had been pushed to the floor, I covered up Anya and then climbed into bed behind her. She moaned softly when I pulled her close, my arm draping over her waist.

Now that the idea had been planted, it began to grow. Anya. Malachi. Me. A trio. A family. And a baby would make four… or five… or six. If she wanted to, we could have as many children as her body could stand. If I could have a little girl with her momma's smile, I think I'd be a happy man. Kissing the top of her head, I had a smile on my face as I whispered. "I can't wait for you to have my babies."

Little did I know, all hell was waiting to break loose. My relationship with Anya was going to be tested in ways I wasn't prepared to deal with.

Seventeen
Anya

I walked into my house after work on Monday, with Malachi in tow, grocery bags in my hands, and my best friend on the phone. Carrie had called just before I got home, so I listened to her as I walked into the kitchen. When she got on a roll, nothing else mattered. She was a good friend—my best friend—but sometimes, she got a one-track mind. Like now.

"Why won't Bryce ask me out again?"

Shaking my head, even though she can't hear me, I put my hand over the microphone and turned to Malachi. "Honey, take off your shoes for momma."

"Anya, are you listening to me? How's my little punkin'? Seems like I haven't seen him in forever."

"Yes, I'm listening to you. Your punkin' is doing just fine. Why don't you come over tomorrow night for dinner? We can sit around, gossip about people, and you can tell me all about why you think Bryce isn't interested any longer. Plus, I thought you two were going hot and heavy. Didn't you try to get me and Hunter to go on a double-date with the two of you just the other week?" I pulled the phone away and put it on speaker. Pulling out the food I was going to cook for dinner, I smile to myself. Hunter was supposed to stop by tonight after work, and I wanted to do something nice for him.

"Yeah, well, he hasn't called me in a week. He never picks up when I try to call him. I text him and he always says he's too busy."

My friend was sad, and I could hear it in her voice. That does sound like he's avoiding her. Not sure why he'd do that. Those two seemed like two peas in a pod when they'd first met. Sure, Carrie can be a lot to deal with, especially if you're not used to her unique brand of style. She could be loud and brash, but she was also loving and loyal and a great friend to have by your side. One day, I hoped my friend would find her very own Prince Charming. Based on what she was saying, it sounded like Bryce was not that man for her.

"Damn, I'm sorry, Carrie. Maybe things are just busy for him with work or something. You know how things get. I mean, look at you and your job. When shit gets crazy, I'm lucky to catch you on the phone until things calm down. Remember that time we didn't talk on the phone for more than a month? I mean, I was ready to break down the doors to your company and drag you out. Maybe it's something like that." It could be, but for some reason, I didn't think it was.

"Yeah, maybe. Anyway, enough about me. How are you and Hunter doing?"

Secrets weren't really a thing between the two of us. We literally told each other everything. Held nothing back. But something was preventing me from telling her any of the details from the weekend with Hunter. Not that anything happened that couldn't be shared, but there was something special about this weekend. Intimate. I wanted to keep it to myself for a while longer. She knew we'd left with him because I couldn't go incognito for four whole days, but that didn't mean I had to share everything that happened.

"We're doing good," I said, not mentioning anything specific about this past weekend. Especially with Carrie in her feelings about Bryce's waning interest. It just didn't seem like the time to share with her how amazing the past four days had been. "He's supposed to be coming over for dinner tonight."

"Wow. I can't believe how you two are still going strong. I expected you to walk away from him after that night and never talk to him again."

"Yeah," I agreed. That had been the plan. Go out for one night, have a little fun, then move on with my life the way it had always been. I didn't need a man to complete me. Everything in my life was set up in a certain way to help make things easier on me. Relationships can be complicated, especially when I sometimes pushed people away, hurting them before they hurt me.

"I'm proud of you," Carrie broke through my internal musings.

Somewhat shocked, I stepped closer to the phone sitting on the counter to make sure I heard her. "You are? Why would you be proud of me?"

"Because you're trying again. I don't know what's going to happen between you and Hunter—"

"Shit, you're not alone in that. I'm hopeful, though."

"And that's why I'm proud of you. You could have turned your back on something—someone—amazing. I always seem to fall for the wrong guy. The ones that should make me run in the other direction as fast as I can."

I almost ran from Hunter and would have kept going in the other direction if he hadn't come after me. That we were even here now was because he was so damn stubborn in the first place. Whatever this was between us was all due to him, and I couldn't be happier.

"Well, this thing between Hunter and me is still so new. I don't really know what to call it at this point. I think it's still too early for me to put a label on it."

"Just don't allow yourself to get hurt. Men like Bryce and Hunter are masters at playing the long game. I know their type. We think we have them figured out and they throw a curveball into the situation. Then we're the ones looking like a fool. I don't want that for you. They usually go for the slim model-types who can cater to their every whim. That's not us. Make you wonder why he's so interested in you, even after Bryce is ghosting me."

My breath stuttered. What was she saying? "Wait a minute. Do you think Hunter is playing games with me? I hope that's not the case. I've already introduced him to Malachi, so if he's not really here for us, then I'm not okay with that." My heart clenched at the thought that Hunter didn't mean all the things he said this weekend. Our connection felt real. When we made love—no, when we had sex—it felt like he was trying to tell me something without words. I needed to stop allowing my thoughts to run wild. Hunter hadn't given me any indication that he wasn't all in with me. That he wasn't serious about pursuing a relationship with me. This was not the time to doubt him.

"No, that's not—I'm sorry, Anya. I'm not saying that at all. You'll have to ignore me. I think I'm a little hurt about Bryce, and I'm projecting my feelings onto Hunter since they're friends." Carrie sighed, and my heart hurt for her. "I'm gonna be fine. Hope you and Hunter and my little man have an amazing dinner tonight. I'm gonna go drown my sorrows in a bottle of wine."

I felt terrible for my friend and wanted to make it better for her. "Want to come over for dinner? I can make enough for four of us. Plus, it would be good for you to get to know Hunter outside of his friendship with Bryce." On the one hand, I wanted her to say yes. I wanted to see her face and make sure she was okay.

On the other hand, things between Hunter and me were still a bit too new, and I wanted this time just for us. Did that make me an awful friend? I hope not. Even so, it didn't change how I felt.

"No, I'm okay. I think I just need to accept that he's not that interested in me." There was a pregnant pause, and I knew she was gearing up to say something else. After being her best friend for almost ten years, I recognized the signs.

"What Carrie?"

"I'm not trying to be funny or anything, but do you see this thing you have with Hunter going far? I mean, from everything I know about him, he's not the type to settle down. You, on the other hand, you want the whole perfect family."

She wasn't saying anything that I hadn't asked myself time and time again. Sure, these past few weeks with Hunter have been amazing, but that didn't mean we'd be together for the long haul. Things happened. People changed. Maybe things would work out with Hunter. Maybe they wouldn't. Either way, I needed to walk into this situation with my eyes wide open and keep them that way.

"Honestly, I'm not sure what's going to happen to us. Right now, I'm just going with the flow. Playing things by ear. We've only been seeing each other for a few weeks."

"Yeah, but you and Malachi went away with him for the weekend."

Rolling my eyes, I regretted telling Carrie about that. Going away for three days without informing someone where we'd be, and with who, was not okay. After all our years of friendship, there was no way I'd go that long without talking to her. Secrets also had a way of coming back to bite you in the ass, so I chose to always be honest. Well, within reason.

"Come on, Carrie. That means nothing. Everything was cool. Hunter did nothing in front of Malachi that would confuse him. We were on our best behavior." What I would not share with Carrie was just how down and dirty we got each night when Malachi went to sleep. Not telling her wasn't a lie. It was just keeping something to myself.

"I'm just looking out for you. You're not the type to go off with a man. It worried me a little. I don't want you to be hurt."

Inexplicably hurt by her words, I snapped. "I'm a grown woman, Carrie. I don't need a babysitter."

Silence.

More Silence.

"I'm sorry, Anya. I know. That's not what I meant."

Carrie was hurt. I could hear it in her tone. The right thing to do in this situation would be to apologize. But I didn't want to. If I put myself in her shoes, I guess I could understand her worry. Typically, I was the conservative and reserved one. When there was a situation that seemed a little too much or we were unsure of how things would play out, I was the voice of reason and calmness. More times than not, I'd been the one to pull Carrie back from doing something crazy. She'd been in love more times than I can count, including that time she fell head over heels for a guitarist in a band who asked her to leave her job and travel the world with him. Yeah, that was a doozy.

That she was the one asking me to slow down and not go too fast with Hunter was... telling.

Maybe I was too close to the situation. It wasn't like me to jump in headfirst, but it felt like Hunter was all I could think about. Not only was he good with Malachi, but he treated me like I was the only woman he needed. In bed and out.

Then again, Carrie had a point. I'd not introduced anyone to Malachi before, let alone taken him with us for a weekend of fun in the sun on a beach. But... Martha's Vineyard. Who wouldn't take the chance to live on the edge a little?

But Carrie was my friend. I know she loved me. She truly cared about me and Malachi. I couldn't be upset with her for doing her best to look out for us. I was about to speak, with Carrie interrupted.

"Alright, well, I'm gonna go. There's a tv show I've wanted to watch."

"Hey, Carrie. I didn't mean to snap at you." I really didn't. It wasn't her fault that I wasn't ready to look too deeply into my relationship with Hunter. If I did, maybe I'd see the cracks forming. Lying to myself had never been a thing for me. From the outside looking in, we didn't match. I knew that. Which brought up the still lingering question of why he wanted to be with me.

He said I was beautiful. Then again, I already knew that, even though I didn't think my looks made me better than anyone else.

We were amazing in bed together. Just thinking about how Hunter made me feel had my body heating up from the inside out.

Malachi liked him. And if I were honest, that counted for more than the two previous things. My baby was all I had in this world. He loved me unconditionally, just as I did him. If he liked Hunter, that meant he had to be a good guy. Babies and puppies were the ultimate tests of a man's character, and Hunter had passed with flying colors. Even so, why did I still have this feeling that I didn't really know who he was?

"It's okay, Anya. I need to learn when to keep my mouth shut. You go cook dinner for my godson. I'll call you tomorrow."

At the click of the phone, I stood in the kitchen looking down at the device in my hand. Although I wouldn't call that an argument, it had been tense. Maybe there was something else going on with Carrie that I didn't know about. Her question made me think. What was truly happening between Hunter and me? Were we just hanging out casually, or were we moving toward something more significant? Yes, I know what he said to me while we were away, but actions speak louder than words.

"Momma?"

Turning, I saw my baby walking over to me and bent over to give him a kiss on his baby fat cheeks. "Yes, sweetheart."

"Hunter," he said, eyes big and sad.

Yeah, I miss him too. It had been less than twenty-four hours, and Malachi and I were both thinking of the one man who could make it better. "Hunter will be here for dinner. First, let's get you out of those clothes so mommy can cook dinner. Okay?"

"Okay," he responded with a smile as I scooped him up in my arms.

As we made our way back to his bedroom, I couldn't help the thought running through my head that I didn't know Hunter as well as I should. Hopefully, when he came over tonight, I'd be able to talk with him about it.

Eighteen
Hunter

Sitting in the bar at Bachelor Tower, I scrolled through my phone, responding to emails from the office. Since I was meeting Anya tonight for dinner at her house, I left early to pick up a few things. Looking at me now, you'd never know I'd been on a tear this morning. After the weekend away, I was ready for the battle waiting for me this morning when I walked into the office. Not only was I pissed that the owner of the software company was trying to play hardball, but his actions had interrupted my time with Anya and Malachi. That's the kind of shit that got under my skin.

I was supposed to be dealing with professionals, not kids trying to sit at the big boy table.

No matter. They found out real fast that I was not the man they wanted to play with. My business was my life. I'd built it with my own two hands. My blood, sweat, and... Nah, fuck that. There weren't any tears involved, but I put in a fuck-ton of effort into this. It was my legacy to leave this world. It was how I'd retired my mother and had her living in a little cottage in Narragansett, as she played card games like Bridge and Gin Rummy with her friends.

No one would fuck with that.

Turns out, my tactic of having their company's reputation ruined worked better than I expected. As soon as I walked into my offices this morning, I received a call from my good friend Conall. Seems the word on the street was that Versus, LLC, the company I was dealing with, was *persona non grata*. They'd been trying to court other companies and playing us against each other. As soon as I gave Dan the order on Friday to block everything they were doing and get the word out that their product was flawed, it spread like wildfire. Within twenty-four hours, every company they'd been talking to pulled out of the negotiations. No matter how much they discounted the price of their software. Clients called to cancel orders by the dozens. Their footprint on the market disappeared almost overnight.

Conall shared with me that he had it on good authority, probably one of the other three O'Shea brothers, that Versus was scrambling. Their company was spiraling. If someone didn't step in to save them, they'd cease to exist in thirty days.

Lifting my drink, I smiled at the memory of that conversation. I'm positive Conall played a hand in things moving so fast. When we'd met a few years ago, there was something about him that resonated with me. On the outside, he was all business, but there was something darker that I could see in his eyes. It was a look I'd seen in the mirror every morning since I'd turned sixteen. He was a man of action, someone who would do whatever it takes to protect himself, his business, and his family. Although Conall's was a bit dirtier than mine from what I'd come to understand, we were cut from the same cloth. I didn't question him about his brothers, but I also knew having Conall in my circle of trust would open doors for me that were once closed. And you're damn right, I stepped through every single one of them.

Lifting my head, I looked around the room and saw a few of the men I'd come to know over the years. One man I didn't know very well, but who had an apartment on the same floor as me, walked over. We didn't have any dealings with each other, so I wasn't really in the mood for a chit-chat.

"Hunter…" he opened.

"Phil, right?" I knew his fucking name, but since I didn't understand why he was coming up to me, he wouldn't have the satisfaction of knowing that.

He sat down in the chair across from me. Adjusting his pants legs, he crossed one foot over his knee. Now I was fucking annoyed. Didn't he see I was busy? Okay, sure, I was looking at my phone while sitting here with a drink. But this motherfucker didn't know me like that. We'd sit here in silence before I acknowledged him again. If he wanted to speak to me about something, he needed to open his fucking mouth.

"Haven't seen you around much."

Turning my head to look at him, I said nothing for a few seconds. Sizing him and dismissing him just that quickly. When did he start tracking my comings and goings? Staring at him, I placed my phone face down on my lap. And waited.

"Last time I saw you was just about one month ago. You were with that beautiful black woman. What was her name again?"

This motherfucker. "Mine."

Phil smirked, and I knew he understood exactly what the fuck I meant.

"Now, come on, Hunter. I mean, isn't that a little old school? You can't just claim a woman as yours. I'm sure she has a name. When I see her again, I'd like to know what to call her."

I could feel my body tense as anger rushed through me. It didn't matter if he'd seen me with Anya once or one hundred times. That he was sitting here in front of me talking this bullshit pissed me off. Glancing down at my watch, I saw the time. Two hours until I was supposed to see them again, but I knew I couldn't wait.

"Watch yourself, Phil. I don't take kindly to threats. There's no reason for you to know her name. You have all the information you need. I'd be careful to keep it that way."

A snarky smile came over his face. "You know, it was just interesting. When she exited your apartment that morning," he paused. "I'm the one who walked her out."

I sprung up from my chair, my phone falling to the floor, as I lunged at him. My hands around his throat as I choked the fucking life out of him. How dare this motherfucker even think about Anya. She's mine. No one dared touch what was mine. I'd fucking kill him first and remove that fucking smirk from his face.

"Hunter," I heard Bryce yelling my name. "Man, you gotta stop."

There weren't many people around this early in the afternoon. Most were still at work. Of course, Bryce's ass was here.

"Fuck that. This motherfucker's over here talking shit. I'm gonna make sure he knows his place," I growled.

"Yeah, but his face is turning blue. If you don't let go, you're gonna kill him. I'm sure you don't want to end up in jail because of this asshole."

His words broke through the red haze. If I was arrested for killing this stupid ass, I know I'd never see Anya and Malachi again. It wouldn't matter how justified I felt my actions were. I smiled down at Phil. "Don't ever come at me again. If you see me in the same room as you, turn the fuck around and leave. Next time, I'll make sure no one else is around." Releasing my hands from around his neck, I stepped back.

"As I said, her name is *Mine*. Remember that shit before I have to give you another lesson."

Bryce held my phone in his outstretched hand, a lopsided smile on his face. "Does she know how you feel?"

Still seething, I couldn't appreciate the tone of his voice. "Why? You got something to say about her, too?"

Hands up, he took a step back. Smiling, he shook his head. "Hell no. Just wondering if she understands how serious you are about her. I liked her. Her friend, not so much. But your woman," he paused, looking over at Phil, who was rubbing the skin along his neck, "well, she seems like the right woman for you." Just as I was about to respond, another voice entered the conversation.

"Phil? Baby, what happened to you?"

Glancing up at the woman standing next to Phil, I shook my head. "You have to be shitting me?" Turning my gaze to Phil. "You like my sloppy seconds? Is that what this is about?" Looking at the blonde rubbing along his face, and making cooing noises to a grown ass man, I smirked. "Hello, Christina. Long time no see."

Her green eyes glared at me. "What did you do to him? Was this over me?"

Bryce laughed loudly, and I couldn't help but roll my eyes. "Fuck this shit. You two deserve each other. Phil, don't forget my warning, motherfucker."

Wheezing, he responded. "Fuck you, Hunter."

"I don't do sloppy seconds. I'll leave that to you." Turning to leave, I looked over at Bryce, who still had a smile on his face.

"You know there are going to be questions about this, right? He's not going to stay quiet."

"Fuck him. I'm not worried." Giving him a half-hug, slap on the back, I began to make my way out.

"I was coming down to have a drink with you, man. Catch up."

I motioned over my shoulder. "No time today, but let's set up something for later this week. I'm headed out to see my lady." At his nod, I continued toward the front of the building.

"Hunter! Hunter!"

What the fuck did she want? I kept walking because there was nothing for us to say.

Christina ran up to me, getting in my way. I shifted to move around her, and she moved as well. Unless I wanted to physically move her, which is not something I would do, I'd need to let her say her peace. "Why are you chasing after me?"

"What was that about with Phil? Did he tell you we were dating? Is that why you were upset?" She walked up to me, placing her hand on my chest.

"Don't touch me," I snarled as I stepped back.

Not getting the message, she stepped closer. "I miss you. Don't you miss me?"

Shaking my head, I could feel a headache coming over me. This is the type of bullshit I didn't need. "No, I don't miss you. We fucked, Christina. That's all. You and I had fun a couple of times, but that's it. Go back to Phil. He seems to be more your speed."

"But I thought...."

The look on her face made me laugh. "Did you think dating Phil would somehow make me jealous? You and I have had nothing to do with each other in almost six months after I caught you leaving your shit in my apartment. It was one night, and you tried to stake your claim on me. You knew that shit didn't fly." Glancing down at my watch, I looked at her again. I had no idea why I was still standing here. Maybe I didn't want to make another scene. Maybe I didn't want to see a woman cry. Either way, "Time's up, Christina. I have someplace to be."

"I'm going to get you back," she whispered as I stepped to the side.

"No. You won't." Her wide eyes and open mouth let me know she thought I hadn't heard her.

Making my way through the lobby and to the elevators to head down to the garage, I couldn't believe how this day was turning out. I went from closing one of the biggest deals of my company and paying a fraction of the original price to almost killing Phil's sorry ass for insinuating he'd be seeing my Anya again. Then being confronted by a former...

acquaintance who was trying to make me jealous.

The only woman that could make me jealous was Anya. Hell, I wasn't even sure when or how it happened. But I know this weekend solidified my feelings for her. No one would get in the way of us being together. If they thought I was an asshole at business, just try to fuck with my relationship.

Finally arriving in the garage, I fired up my car and exited the building. I just needed to keep my cool when I arrived at her house. This wasn't a side of me that I wanted her to show her or Malachi. Not that I was hiding who I was from her. It was more that I needed her to see the man who only wanted her in life, not the one who would wrap his hands around the neck of a man who pissed me off. That version of me was not someone I ever wanted to touch the lives of Anya and Malachi. As long as people stayed in their place, my two lives would never touch, and I meant to keep it that way.

Nineteen
Hunter

Forty-five minutes later, I arrived at Anya's house. On the way, I stopped by the local toy store for Malachi. There was no way I was stepping over that threshold without a toy for my little buddy. Then I stopped by a boutique jewelry store. It wasn't time for the big purchase just yet, but I wanted to grab Anya a small token of my affection. Buying gifts for the women I dated wasn't my usual thing. Then again, all my old ways were slowly disappearing. Nothing about dating Anya was going to plan.

I couldn't help but chuckle at my life now. Stepping out of my car, I hoisted the bags filled with all the goodies I'd picked up for them on my way over. The door opened as I was walking up the driveway.

"Hunter, you're early." She stood in the door looking beautiful. It wasn't that she was trying to entice me. She wore shorts, a t-shirt, her feet bare, and her hair in a ponytail. But to me, it didn't matter because she was gorgeous no matter what she had on.

She was stunning. I knew she'd challenge that notion if she knew what I was thinking. It didn't change the facts. Suddenly, a vision of Anya waiting for me to come home at the end of the day began playing in my mind. My lips lifted in a smile at the thought. It felt good. It felt right. Whenever I thought about my future, it ever included a wife and children. It just wasn't what I wanted for my life... until her.

"I couldn't wait to see you," I responded, stepping closer and leaning down to kiss her softly. "Hello, beautiful."

Anya smiled, tucking a few strands of hair behind her ear. "Man, stop lying. You know I look like a hot mess." She moved to the side, opening the door wider for me to step through. "Malachi will be happy to see you. He's been asking about you since we got home. I wasn't sure if you were gonna bail on me."

Closing the door behind me, I followed her as she walked into the living room. "I'd never bail on purpose. Plus, you know I would have called if something had come up. Seeing the two of you has become the best part of my days." Watching the sway of her hips, I bit my lip. This woman made me want her more every single day. Even when she wasn't trying to turn me on, she did. It was more than just her beauty, but it was the way she looked at me. Those brown eyes of hers brought me to my knees. When she looked at me after we made love, all I wanted to do was keep her wrapped up in my arms. If I went more than a few hours without talking to her or even receiving a text message with one of those silly memes, I got antsy. She'd become such a huge part of my life. I wasn't sure what I'd do if something changed that. Removing my suit jacket, I rolled up my shirtsleeves. I wasn't going anywhere but here, so I may as well relax. "Need any help?"

"Have you eaten?"

"No, not yet."

"Good," she turned to look at me. "I was planning to make spinach ravioli."

"My favorite."

"I know," she sighed. "Just thought it was time I do something special for you. I can't whisk you away for a weekend at Martha's Vineyard or anything like that…."

Coming closer to her, I wrapped my arms around her waist. "I don't need you to do those things. What I do for you is because I want to. Nothing I do needs reciprocity. Spending time with you, and Malachi, is all I need. You give me things money can't buy. That's what I need right now." I leaned down to kiss her soft lips. "That you would make my favorite meal as a token of affection means a lot to me."

More than she'll ever know. It was the meal my mother would make for us when times were good. When my deadbeat father was locked up in jail and the threat of him coming home in a drunken stupor and hitting on her, she'd been happy and free. Just me, her, and Caleb. Those weren't the things I'd spoken to Anya about, so her gesture meant even more to me. She wasn't doing this for any other reason than I'd told her it was one of my favorite meals. To others, it would be small. To me, it meant everything.

She sighed before laying her head on my chest. "I sometimes feel things are so lopsided.

You do so much for us. You come over after work, even when you're worn down from the day. It's like you're constantly catering to us."

"Because I want to. Do you think I'd be here if I didn't want to be? That I'd spend so much time with the two of you if you weren't important to me?"

Delving deeper into my feelings wasn't an option for me. Not right now. Plus, after the situation with Phil, things were too close to the surface. I didn't want to react too soon or say something I shouldn't. Was I intentionally ignoring how I felt about Anya? Damn right I was. I'd face the reality of what we were doing later. Right now, all I wanted to do was hold Anya close to me. Never let her go.

"Hunter!"

Well, except for when my little man was around. Releasing Anya, I turned and scooped Malachi into my arms. "Hey, buddy. Did you miss me?"

He nodded. "Yes."

Glancing back at Anya, who had a huge smile on her face, I couldn't help but pull her forward, wrapping my arms around my two favorite people. This is where I belonged. With all the other mess that regularly surrounded me, standing in Anya's kitchen had given me the most peace that I've had in years.

"Hunter?" Malachi called my name.

"Yeah, buddy?"

"Hungry. Chicken nuggets?"

This kid had a one-track mind. Glancing over at Anya, I knew she wouldn't let him get away with it today, and for once, I was on her side. It was time to expand this little guy's palate. "Hungry? Yes. Chicken nuggets? No. Not tonight. Your mom is making something special for me tonight."

"Yuk, Hunter. Chicken nuggets," he demanded.

"Nope. You deal with him. I'm not doing this with him tonight," Anya said as she stepped back from me. "If you want to handle that conversation, feel free. I'm going to begin dinner so I can feed this little monster." Leaning over, she kissed Malachi's forehead and tickled his side, causing him to laugh.

The sound of his joy stunned me. Today, his laughter hit me differently. With my new perspective, I glanced over at the young boy. I'd do everything in my power to make sure I heard this sound every day. Turning my gaze to Anya, I smiled down at her. Before she had a chance to fully step away, I grabbed her hand, pulling her back. "Thank you," I whispered as I placed a kiss on her lips.

She canted her head to the side in confusion. "You're welcome. But what are you thanking me for?"

So many words ran through my head. I wanted to thank her for welcoming me into her home and into her life. For allowing me to get to know her and Malachi. For giving so freely of herself even when I demanded more. But those are the things I wasn't ready to say just yet.

"For being you."

"Awwww, thank you. But I don't know any other way to be." Stepping away, she moved toward the refrigerator. "Now, you two go away and get out of my hair. I have some stuff to do."

I looked at Malachi. "Your momma wants us to go play."

"Okay. Bye, momma."

We weren't going more than twenty feet away from his mother.

"Bye, baby. Dinner will be ready in thirty minutes. Can you hold out?" This was directed at me.

"We'll be fine."

As I walked into the living room, Malachi in my arms, I wondered what my life would be like if I'd taken the usual route. Where I would be if I hadn't been so focused on building a legacy for myself. Would I have a wife at this point in my life? A son or daughter? Sitting Malachi down on the couch as I sat, I knew I was only torturing myself. The choices I'd made were the best for me at the time. I didn't regret my life. If I sometimes lost myself in the darkness, in the arms of women who meant nothing to me, then that was the price I paid. Not anymore. That life was behind me, and I'd do anything to hold on to the future that was in front of me, even if I wasn't quite ready to examine what the changes happening to me really meant.

Turning to Malachi, I watched him play with some superhero toys, making clashing noises as they fought.

"Play?" He asked, and there was no way I could resist giving in. Picking up one of the toys, I began to play superheroes and villains with the little boy who'd stolen my heart, along with his momma.

Thinking back to the situation earlier today at my apartment building, I know if Bryce hadn't been there, I probably would have killed Phil. I wasn't known for losing my shit, but when I did, it was usually epic. He was lucky I let him go with only bruises in the shape of my hands. I'd done more to people for less. That he'd tried to bring Anya into this situation just pissed me off even more. Anya wasn't like the other women in my life. She wasn't someone I'd just walk away from. Neither would I allow anyone to disrespect her. She made me feel something more than the hollow feeling in my gut that had been my constant companion for too many years to count. Just being with her made me want to be a better man for her. Did that mean I would change who I was when it came to my business? No. But then again, my business was separate from what I had here, with her.

"Would you like something to drink? I bought wine for dinner but also broke down and grabbed some of that scotch you like to drink." Anya stood in the entrance to the living room, her body leaned up against the wall separating the kitchen from the living area.

Leaning back against the couch, toys still in my hands, I took her in. My feelings for her were more than I ever thought possible.

"You bought my favorite liquor? The fifteen-year scotch?"

"Yes," she said, fidgeting in front of me.

Anya was nervous. As she should be. Because that shit was expensive.

"Why?" Something inside me needed to know the answer to her question. My heart was beating a mile a minute as I waited for her to speak.

"Because you're important to me. You came into my life and turned my world upside down. I wanted to do something to show you that I pay attention to what matters to you. That's why I'm making your favorite meal tonight." She stepped away from the wall and walked over to me. She sat down on the coffee table in front of me. Her body relaxed, face free of make-up, and toes squirming against the carpet. "I know we're not ready for the words just yet, but you mean... more to me than I expected. When you're near me, everything feels right. When you're gone, I get antsy, nervous for the next time we're going to see each other. Life doesn't always go the way we expect it to, but going out with Carrie was probably one of the best decisions I've made in my life."

As she spoke, I leaned closer to her, placing the toys to the side of me. By the time she'd finished, my hands were cupping her face.

"Baby, you can feel however you want. I feel the same about you. I tried to stay away at the beginning, slow things down."

"How'd that work out for you?" She questioned, laughing.

Gazing into her face, I ran my thumb across her bottom lip. "Not so hot. No matter how much I tried to stay away, all I could think about was being with you. About kissing you. Holding you." I stopped talking and pulled her face closer. "You're mine, Anya." Sliding my tongue across her lips before deepening our contact.

"Ewwww, mommy. No kiss Hunter. He's my Hunter."

Laughing, we broke apart and glanced over at Malachi. His little face was scrunched up in disgust as he stared at us.

"No kiss Hunter, mommy."

"Okay, baby," she said, looking over at her son before capturing my gaze again. "Would you like that drink now?"

"I want more than a drink, but it'll do for now." Releasing her from my grip, I sat back on the couch again. "This isn't over. I'm not going anywhere."

She smiled at me as she stood up again. "Dinner will be ready in another fifteen minutes."

"I can't wait," I winked at her.

Watching her walk away, I smiled. Anya was going to be my wife one day. It would shock the hell out of anyone I knew if they had any inkling that I was thinking this way, but I knew this was what I needed. She was who I needed.

"Here," Malachi's voice called out. "You be the good guy this time."

Was it possible for me to be the good guy? I hadn't been a good guy for a long time now.

Accepting the toy, I stared at it as I continued to roll that question around in my head.

Could I be the good guy?

For Malachi and Anya, I could try.

Twenty
Anya

I walked out of Malachi's room, pulling the door almost closed as he fell asleep. He'd asked for two stories tonight, and I gave in to him. Again. He'd been so wound up from playing with Hunter tonight, he couldn't settle down. Even after a nice serving of spinach ravioli—which he loved—watching two episodes of his favorite show and rolling around on the floor for another thirty minutes.

Making my way down the hallway, I couldn't help the smile that came over my face as I thought about the night we'd had. Just yesterday, we'd been on our way back from Martha's Vineyard after a weekend of fun, sand, and enjoying each other.

In some ways, I still questioned what we were doing. How we could have gotten this close so quickly? Stepping into the living room, I saw Hunter sprawled on the couch, his phone in one hand as he scrolled through whatever information held his attention. Black slacks covered his legs, his blue shirt spread across his chest, his blond hair pulled back in a topknot. My fingers itched to run my fingers through the silky strands. At the thought of being so close to him again, my core began to ache and clench. I missed him being inside of me. Addiction could be a bad thing, except when it came to Hunter Malone.

"Why are you standing there just staring at me?" he asked without lifting his head from the phone.

My body jerked, and I banged my elbow on the wall. "Ow," I yelled out.

His low chuckle sounded across the room. When I looked up, he was staring at me, one arm outstretched. "Come here, beautiful. Let Daddy kiss it better."

And just like that, all the pain was forgotten as I began walking over to him. Hunter had that effect on me. I welcomed it. Before him, I dated a couple of times, but none of them made me feel this way. Hell, none of them had been invited to meet Malachi. That Hunter was here, in my home, was saying more than anything else could.

My call earlier with Carrie floated in my mind. I know it hurt her that Bryce wasn't interested, but that didn't give her any right to question my relationship with Hunter. I couldn't allow myself to get caught up in her drama. Not this time. Stepping in front of Hunter, he looked up at me, his hands coming up to grab my arm before pulling me to sit down on his lap.

"Does it still hurt?" He asked, bringing my arm up to his lips and kissing the spot that I'd been rubbing earlier.

My nipples hardened under my t-shirt. "N-No. It feels fine."

"Are you sure? I'm happy to do whatever I can to make it feel better."

I sighed in supplication before leaning my head against his. "What if I hurt someplace else?"

Cupping my face with one of his large palms, he lifted my head so that we stared into each other's eyes. "Wherever you hurt, I will make it better. If you ache, I'll do whatever I can to soothe you. No matter what you need, I'm here to make you feel better."

"Why are you so good to me?" I couldn't help the question bursting from my lips.

"Because you're mine."

I gasped in surprise and pleasure at his words. My vision blurred as I leaned toward him, capturing his lips in a sensual kiss. "Then that also makes you mine."

In one swift motion, he stood, lifting my body in his arms. "Baby, you just said the magic words."

A giggle escaped as he carried me to my bedroom. It was so odd being in his arms this way. I know it was my own internal issues with my body image, but I never felt comfortable when a man tried to carry me. There was always a feeling that he'd drop me in a heap of limbs on the floor because I was too heavy. With Hunter, that fear was never there. Not once had I ever doubted that he could lift me and carry me around. I felt safe in his arms and secure in the feeling that he would always take care of me.

Dangerous to feel this way about a man so soon in our relationship? Probably. Did I care? No. This felt too good. There was no way I would change one single thing. Once in my bedroom, he placed me down and I stood in front of him.

"Strip."

My hands immediately went to remove my shirt and shorts. Hunter also unbuttoned his shirt, baring his chest to my heated gaze. As he pitched the garment over to the side, I picked up the scent of his cologne. My eyes fluttered closed, and a moan was ripped from my throat. Opening my eyes to look at him, I slid my panties down my body and stood in front of him naked but unafraid. I knew he would take care of me. He always did.

Hunter stepped close to me, his thick rod pressing hot and heavy against my stomach. If I could connect our bodies and never be apart from him, I would. When he kissed me, I leaned in, trying to get even closer to him. He stepped forward. I stepped back. Arriving at the edge of my bed, we climbed on top, my legs widening for him to lie in between.

Tears came to my eyes as I stared up at him. Damn. I loved him.

Such an amateur move on my part, but God help me, I couldn't stop the way I felt. His body pressed against mine, and the intensity of my feelings for Hunter scared me. If only I could say the words to him, but my mouth wouldn't move. I was still holding back from him. I wasn't sure why.

Was I afraid he didn't feel the same? Based on how he treated me, there would be no reason to think he didn't return my feelings.

Was I still thinking about Carrie's accusation that I didn't know him as well as I thought? I shouldn't be, but I know they played a role.

If I said the words, would he lose interest? Honestly, I just didn't know.

His lips on my soft flesh chased those conflicting thoughts out of my head. None of that mattered right now. All I cared about was being with him right now and showing him with my actions exactly how I felt about him. Reaching up, I removed the hairband, his hair releasing to frame his chiseled face.

"You like messing with my hair when I'm inside you. Why is that?" He asked, his voice low and gravelly. I liked to think I was the reason he had trouble speaking.

"Because it reminds me that you're still not ready to be tamed yet. You're still rough. Raw. I like you that way. You're not always the businessman in a suit making million-dollar deals."

Moving one knee, he brought his thick member flush against my slick channel. "Sweetheart, I'm always the businessman making million-dollar deals. But I'm also the man who wants to hear you moan in ecstasy and scream my name as I make you mine."

I felt his lower body rocking, his thick mushroom head tapping at my entrance. It felt so good. Words were hard right now because I just wanted him inside me. The rocking continued as he placed soft kisses along my skin, nipping my flesh along the way.

"I'm not letting you go, Anya."

I sighed. "I don't want you to," I whispered as my hands grabbed him around his waist, pulling him tighter.

"I'm not perfect," he said, as if admitting he'd stolen the Mona Lisa painting from The Louvre.

"Hunter," I moaned. "I don't need you to be perfect. I just need you here with me," I pleaded with him as he began to thrust. He surged inside, causing me to gasp out loud. He quickly covered my mouth with his, covering the sound and distracting me at the same time.

He does this twice, then takes things up a notch. He slams in hard, the feeling so intense, tears spring up in my eyes. My arms tightened around him, my nails scoring against his bare skin. Tensing under my touch for a moment, he continued to thrust forward, and I hold on to him for dear life.

After a few minutes of flailing around like a rag doll underneath him, I meet his thrusts. We lose ourselves in the overwhelming sensations. Electricity is crackling between us, making our connection even more exhilarating. Both of his hands go under me, and he tilts my lower body up, giving him a different angle. I can feel my sheath gripping him tightly. My stomach clenches as my body prepares for my release. We break our kiss. His mouth immediately latches onto the skin between my neck and shoulder. I'm confident he will leave a love bite, and I don't have the energy to care.

There's no way I'm stopping him. Everything I feel for him is so overwhelming.

"Oh, Hunter," I can't help but moan as I careen towards the precipice.

"That's it, baby. Hold on tight. Don't let me go. I want you addicted to me, to the feel of me inside you," he says, slamming into me again and again.

I can feel the spasms come over me as my channel clenches tight. As my mouth drops open in a silent scream, I feel the tingles go through me. My toes curled as my legs tighten around him. "Oh, fuck."

"Give it to me. I want it all," Hunter growled, his voice rough.

He slams faster, harder, losing control as he meets me where I'm already at. Another orgasm rushes through me, and I'm so ready for it. I want this feeling to never stop. I want him to never stop being inside me. Everything he's giving me feeds my soul, and I need it now more than ever. My hips lift as I meet him thrust for thrust. He's not in this alone. He claimed me, and I'm claiming his ass right back.

I can feel the waves of ecstasy in every part of my body. In the back of my mind, I can hear him roar out his release, and all I can do is smile because I know he's just as lost as I am.

No one else could take his place. I'm ruined for any other man, not that I need anyone other than Hunter. He came into my life like a damn wrecking ball and obliterated every objection I had. Every time I put up a wall to us moving forward, he crushed it, eliminating every excuse I had that would prevent us from being right here, together.

As we take a few minutes to catch our breath, he remains inside me. I love him. I'll never admit it out loud because I still have Malachi to think about, but I don't see how any man can take Hunter's place. And I'll be damned if I give him up to another woman without a fight. I guess that settles it then.

"Stay," I whisper to him.

He looks down at me. I've never asked him to stay over before. Usually, I make sure he leaves during the night so that Malachi won't wake up to find us in bed together. Tonight is the beginning of a new journey for us. No more hiding what we mean to each other. I'm sure I've caught him off-guard with my request, but his silence is unnerving. "Say something, Hunter."

Suddenly, a smile lit up his face. "Yes, Anya," he says before moving to the side. "I'd love nothing more." He grabs me around the waist, pulling me closer. With my back pressed against his chest, he places a soft kiss on my shoulder. "You're never going to get rid of me now."

I try to hide my smile. "Yeah, Mr. Malone, that's kinda the idea."

"Then it's a good idea that I had no plans to go anywhere."

As I snuggle in closer, I hope I'm not taking a leap off a tall bridge. Being with someone like Hunter is scary enough. The last thing I want to do is give my heart to him, and he tramples all over me. Then again, I know that Hunter would never do that to me. I can trust him.

With that thought, I close my eyes and fall asleep, comforted by the knowledge that I've finally found my prince charming.

Twenty-One
Anya

I rechecked my face in the bathroom mirror as I waited for Carrie to come out of the stall. Malachi was spending the night with my parents, so I wanted to make the night special for Hunter and me. He'd been coming to my place pretty much since we met, and I wanted to be back on his turf. Since that first night he'd spent at my house, he'd been there every night. No matter what time he got off work, he made his way to us. But I didn't want him to think this was a one-way street. He gave to me all the time, and I wanted him to know we were in this together.

Friday was finally here, the long week was over, and now it was time to spend some time with my man. We would have drinks at his apartment building before heading out for a night on the town. I was positive we'd end up back here at his place, and I was looking forward to it.

My freedom ticket was good until noon tomorrow, and I would take full advantage of grandparents wanting to see their grandson and spoil him rotten.

"I wonder if Bryce will be with him," she said, a huge smile on her face.

Staring at my friend in the bathroom mirror, I cringed a little. Hunter didn't know Carrie was going to join me tonight. Not sure what he would have said if he did. Although she wasn't going out with us when we left, I was bringing along a third wheel. Yeah, I know. Not cool.

After our intense conversation on Monday, she'd called me at work on Tuesday to explain why she'd been so emotional. For her, Bryce was the perfect man. Attentive. Handsome. Made her feel special. She'd really thought he was the perfect man for her. At least until he pulled back.

Of course, I felt sorry for my friend. It wasn't my place to get involved in her romantic relationships, just like I didn't need her involved in mine, which I made clear to her. Hunter was not Bryce, and whatever happened between the two of us was something that I'd deal with in my own way. If we didn't work out, it would be because it wasn't the right time for us, or if one of us did something stupid. As of today, he'd given me no reason to distrust him.

"Carrie," I turned to her. "Listen, I know you think showing up here is the right thing to do so that you and Bryce can talk, but now that we're here. I'm not sure this is the right idea. I'm just worried about how things will look if you go out there and Bryce isn't expecting it."

"What do you mean? I thought you were on my side," she whined, her eyes glistening in the harsh overhead lights.

"Come on, Carrie. Don't be like that. Of course, I'm on your side. You know I always have your back. I'm just..." I paused and looked at her face. My stomach twisted.

I haven't shared with Carrie that I don't think tonight will turn out the way she thinks. I'm worried she's going to get her heartbroken. But I also understand. She wants something more than what her life is right now. From the outside looking in, she has everything she needs to be a success. A fantastic job, more money than she knows what to do with, and me as her best friend, which was a pretty good damn deal, if you asked me.

That ex-husband of hers had really done a job on her confidence and self-esteem. During the divorce proceedings, she found out he'd been cheating on her from the very beginning. Even had a child with another woman that he'd been hiding, basically living two separate lives. So, yeah, I completely understood why she'd latch on to Bryce. I was just worried things would get worse before they got better.

"You know what, Carrie? Don't listen to me. I'm sure everything's going to be fine. Are you ready?"

Carrie nodded. "As ready as I'm going to be. By the way, you look amazing tonight. Hunter isn't going to know what hit him when he sees you."

Pulling my short skirt down to cover more of my thighs, I fidgeted a little. This dress was so unlike me, but I wanted to go all out. The plunging scoop neckline, the shimmery red material, and the too-short skirt were meant to entice. At least that's what the woman who sold it to me said as I handed over my credit card. We'll see if it has the desired effect.

"Girl, stop making me nervous. Come on."

Exiting the bathroom, we made our way towards the lounge. Things really seemed to be hopping tonight because as we walked toward the bar entrance, there was a line of scantily clad women walking in front of them. Of course, I knew this was the place to be if you wanted to meet a handsome, rich man. Then again, who knew they came out in droves? As Carrie and I walked inside, I immediately glanced around, looking for Hunter.

This time, I noticed the looks from the other men in the room. Their eyes followed us as we walked into the elegant space. I'm not gonna lie, they were all fine as hell, but none of them could compare to the man I was here to see. Hunter had repeatedly shown me exactly what I meant to him. Neither of us had said the words yet, but my feelings for him were laid bare every time I looked at him. Every time I lay with him, cradled in his firm embrace, all I want to do is stay there with him. To never let him go. Poker was never my game of choice, so I know my emotions are all over my face, even though I tried to hide.

The crowd was too dense, and I wasn't trying to walk around searching for him. Plus, I needed a drink. Touching Carrie's arm, I motioned towards the bar. "Hey, let's grab a drink." At her nod, we made our way over. I gave my order to the bartender. "Dirty Martini, bleu cheese olives."

Carrie made her order as well. "The same thing, please. And let me have a few extra olives."

As he left to go make the drinks, we stood facing each other. It felt as if we stood out. Maybe because we weren't on the prowl for any man. Both Carrie and I were focused only on our men. Well, I was focused on my man. Carrie was hoping to stake her claim. Looking around, I watched the mating game being played and almost laughed. The women flipping their hair and batting their eyelashes at the men who sized them up like an expensive piece of steak.

"Do you see them?" Carrie peered around as I tried to ignore all the people mixing and mingling.

The bartender dropped off our drinks, and I passed one glass to Carrie. "Thank you," I said before placing some money on the bar. I wasn't going to be here long, so there was no need to start a tab.

"I wonder if Bryce would get jealous if I hooked up with one of the men here," Carrie said with a wicked smile.

Shaking my head, I glanced over at her. The gleam in her eyes told me she was up to something. I was positive that I didn't want any part of it. "Girl, you better be careful. You're playing a dangerous game."

Flipping her hair, she smiled at me. "I mean, why should I wait around for Bryce to get his shit together? I know I'm a catch, but if he's too stupid to recognize that, then that's his loss."

"Are you sure?" I questioned. "You kinda had your eyes set on him."

Carrie nodded. "Time for me to move on, right? Just look around us. There are probably thirty men in this room. All of them are rich. All of them sexy. Why should I limit myself and chase after a man who doesn't want me? That's not my style."

Sipping my drink, I smiled over at her. "Well, I'm happy you've decided to move on. If Bryce can't recognize how fabulous you are, then you don't need him in your life."

"Yes, exactly," Carrie said, flipping her long blonde hair over her shoulder.

This was what I'd hoped for tonight. Yes, I know bringing her along without letting Hunter know wasn't cool, but this was my girl, and she needed some cheering up. As I noticed the crowd clearing up, I looked over to the right and noticed someone who I thought was Hunter. Because of so many people around, I could only see the back of his head. "Hey, I think I see Hunter. You ready?"

Carrie nodded. "Yeah, give me just one second." She took another big sip and ate an olive. "Okay, now I'm ready."

Just as we were about to step away, a guy came into our space.

"Hey. Never thought I'd see you again. Remember me?"

Glancing up at him, it took me a minute to remember his face. As soon as I did, I could feel my face heat with embarrassment. "Oh. Um. Aren't you the guy who helped me leave that morning?"

His smile was overly large and a tad creepy. He stepped closer to me. I took a step back. Sure, I'd met him once for a brief moment over a month ago, but something about him was making me uneasy.

"Yeah. I'm Phil. You're Anya, right?" He paused, holding out his hand to me. "It's very good to see you again."

Did I give him my name when we met? Things were a bit fuzzy from that morning. Of course, that was over a month ago. So much had happened since that day. Even still, I wasn't really trying to speak with him. Reaching out my hand to him, I tried to quickly return the gesture. When I pulled away, he held tighter. Yes, I appreciated what he'd done for me, but my focus was on getting over to Hunter. "Um…" I honestly wasn't sure how to answer, but I was saved by the proverbial bell.

"Let's go, Anya," Carrie called out. "I think I see him."

I knew the 'him' was one of two people, either Hunter or Bryce. Jerking my hand away from Phil's grasp, I turned to Carrie. "Then let's go."

"Where are you running off to? I thought we could talk a bit more." Phil stepped into my space. I paused before taking a step back.

"I'm here to meet someone."

Suddenly, his face contorted. "Ah yes, Hunter," he snarled. "Well, let me know if you need another escort from the building after he's finished with you."

What the fuck? "Excuse the fuck outta you?" That creepy feeling from earlier became stronger. Clearly, he had an issue with Hunter, but that was not my problem. If he has a problem with my man, then he needed to take it up with him. Leave me the hell out of it.

He held up the hand that wasn't holding the drink, as if trying to play it off. "No. No. Just offering my services to a beautiful lady. You know how men who live here can be. Once the night is over, sometimes we forget to be a gentleman. You'd never have to worry about that with me."

Yeah, I was done with this motherfucker. Turning to Carrie, I tipped my head. "Come on."

She gave Phil a dirty look as she moved to walk away. "You may be cute, but your attitude sucks."

The man had to nerve to smile and tip his drink at us. "Enjoy your night, ladies."

As we moved through the crowd, I glanced over my shoulder at Phil, who was staring at us as we walked away. "What the fuck is his problem?" I said under my breath.

"Jealousy. He said you met him before when you were here. What's that about?"

"When I left Hunter's apartment that morning, he was the one who escorted me out of the building. At the time, I thought nothing of it. Now, I wonder."

"Are you gonna tell Hunter?"

That was a big ass negative. "No. As long as he doesn't come into my space again, I'll leave it alone. Weird as fuck, right?"

"You got that right," Carrie responded. Then she stopped in her tracks, and I almost ran into her back.

I stepped to the side, glancing at her. "What happened? You alright?"

She looked at me. Her eyes held a look of sadness. "Um, maybe we should go back to the bar."

"Why should we do that?" Moving to walk in front of her, I lifted my head and saw what she was looking at. Or should I say *who* she was looking at?

Hunter.

With another woman.

Her arms wrapped around his waist. Their lips pressed together in a kiss.

"Fuck. I think I'm going to be sick," I said just before I turned to leave. Get out. That was the only thought running through my mind. Water filled my eyes as my heart broke. Of course, he was too good to be true. He knew I was coming here tonight and still had the unmitigated gall to be wrapped up in the arms of another woman.

I stopped. I would not run away like a coward. I wasn't the one who did something wrong. That was all Hunter. If this is how he wanted to play the situation, then I'd make sure he knew I was fully aware of the game.

Turning back, I saw they were now separated. Storming over in their direction, I stood facing them. The blonde woman turned to me with a smirk on her face before wiping one thumb across her lipstick smeared mouth. My gaze focused on Hunter, and I'm sure the look in my eyes was a little crazed. Then again, who could blame me? Not only had he betrayed my trust, but he'd also broken my heart. "Want to explain to me why you were kissing another woman when you were in my bed this morning?"

Twenty-Two
Hunter

As I look around the room, I have the sudden realization that this life is no longer appealing to me. Meeting Anya was a turning point in my life. She is someone I needed, but now that she's in my life, I can't see myself without her. And Malachi.

This was going to be a special night for us, and I was ready to take things to the next level. This past week, spending the night at her house helped me see what I wanted for my future. The bachelor life was all well and good, but it was time for me to move toward something different. It was hard as hell to get an apartment here, but once a man got married, he had to leave. There was no other choice. I know the new owner had tried to change things up by testing out having women live in the building, but that didn't work out the way it was supposed to.

Plus, I no longer felt this place served my needs. It has served its purpose for the time I'd been here. Glancing down at my watch, I noted the time. Anya would be here in another thirty minutes. My woman wanted to surprise me, which I was all for. Earlier today, I'd received a text from her letting me know she was leaving work early to prepare for dinner tonight at Ocean Prime. I'd been there a few times for business meetings. Anya mentioned she'd never eaten there, but it was on her restaurant wish list.

Tonight was all about her and what she wanted. My only thought was making sure she knew just how much she meant to me. That what we were building—my relationship with her—was more than just a moment of fun for me. She was the One. If that meant it was time for me to make some changes in my life, then that's how it would have to be.

"Fancy meeting you here."

I sighed. Not tonight. This was not what I needed. Glancing down at my watch, I saw that Anya was supposed to arrive in about twenty minutes. All I needed to do was get Christina the hell away from me before Anya showed up. Looking up at her, I shook my head in disbelief.

"Keep walking, Christina. We have nothing to say to each other. Why don't you go find your new man and leave me alone?" Some would say my words were too harsh. They weren't. This woman couldn't take a fucking hint. She constantly showed up in my vicinity, like a bad fucking penny.

"Don't tell me what to do," she snapped at me with her lips pulled back, teeth bared, and eyes wide.

Then, in the blink of an eye, she regained her composure, slipping the mask back on. If I hadn't been paying attention, I wouldn't have noticed the transformation.

She looked around the room. Searching for someone. When a smile came over her face, I thought she'd found who she was waiting for and would leave soon. I was mistaken. As she stood in front of me, I stayed silent. It was better that I do not engage her in any way. Anything I said to her, she would use against me. According to many, I was a bastard who didn't care about anyone, but I honestly did not enjoy treating women poorly. Business was something different. With matters of the heart, I did my best to tread lightly. I know that my choices, and the way I've lived my life, weren't the same choices others would make. I have no regrets, but I know others judged me for the way I handled things.

Tired of sitting and having her look down on me, I stepped out into the lobby and wait for Anya to arrive. If I stayed here any longer, I was bound to say something that would only make things worse for both of us. Plus, there were too many damn people in this place tonight. Even when Anya arrived, she'd have a hard time finding me in the crush of people. We'd planned to have a drink here, then head over to the restaurant. Now that Christine had shown up, I've changed my mind. We'd have drinks at the restaurant.

Placing my phone inside my inner coat pocket, I stood. "If you'll excuse me," I tried again to be polite.

"Why won't you talk to me, Hunter? Wasn't I good to you?" Christina stepped closer.

At one point, she would have been everything I wanted in a woman, but when I compare her to Anya, I find her lacking in every area. I'm sure some other man would find

Christina perfect. As for me, the only woman I wanted by my side had mahogany brown skin, naturally curly hair, a small stomach pooch that she constantly tried to hide from me, an ass that could make a grown man cry, and the sounds she made while I made love to her was my nightly lullaby. Fuck, I could feel my cock thicken in my pants as I pictured Anya this morning. Wild hair, swollen lips, love bites covering her breasts, sweat covering her body, and a smile on her face. That was my woman. The only woman for me.

"I'm with someone else now. You knew the deal and tried to change things because I fucked you good. That was over seven months ago. That you can't move the fuck on is not my problem. Talking to you is not my concern. Now, I said excuse me, so I'd like you to step out of my way."

For a moment, I saw the person from earlier. The angry woman who wouldn't let things go. She glanced away for a second. When she turned back to me, her smile was back. What the fuck was up with this woman? Suddenly, she stepped close to me, wrapping her arms around my waist and planting her mouth against mine. Even I hadn't expected this, so yes, it took me a moment to respond. Within seconds, I pushed her away and wiped my hand across my lips.

"What the fuck are you doing?" I hissed at her. "You must want to get banned, because you know that shit isn't cool. Don't ever touch me again."

"I just wanted to remind you of how good we are together."

"Want to explain to me why you were kissing another woman when you were in my bed this morning?"

"Anya." I knew immediately what she'd seen and what she was thinking. "Sweetheart, this isn't what you think." As she stared at me,

I could see her eyes glistening, and I prayed she wouldn't let the tears fall. Moving toward her, I reached my hand out. "Baby, come on. You know I wouldn't kiss another woman."

She shook her head. "Do I know that, Hunter? Because from where I'm standing, it sure as hell looks like you had your lips planted against hers."

Christina picked the worst moment possible to open her big mouth. "Who are you? We were having a private moment." Was she serious? Staring at her, I noticed the smirk on her face, and the pieces all fell together. She'd planned this. When she'd been looking around earlier, she'd been searching for Anya. If Christina knew who Anya was, someone she'd never seen before, then that meant someone else was involved. My eyes landed on Phil standing off to the side. The bastard had the nerve to smile and lift his glass in a toast. I'd have to deal with him later. Right now, I had an angry girlfriend on my hands.

"Anya, let's go."

"No. I came with Carrie," she motioned behind us. "Good thing I did, right? Because who knew I'd find my boyfriend kissing…" Anya glared at Christina before shaking her head, "someone like this."

"Hey!" Christina gasped. "At least I look like the type of woman he deserves to have by his side."

That was it! "Are you fucking kidding me, Christina? Go away. This is not your concern. You kissed me when I wasn't expecting it. You're lucky my lady doesn't knock you on your ass. If you were smart, you'd leave now before shit gets even messier. But know this, I won't forget what you did here tonight." I looked over at Phil. "Neither of you. You're going to pay for this little show you put on. I can guarantee you that."

"Hunter, you can't mean that," she said with a pout on her face.

Anya shifted her body so that she was facing Christina. "If he doesn't, I do. This is a nice place, and I don't want to do anything to embarrass myself. But if you don't step the fuck away from my man, I won't be responsible for what happens next."

"You're nobody to him," Christina spat. "When he's finished playing with the reject, he'll come back to me.

The look on Anya's face made me smile. I'd never seen her this way, but I had to admit it was kinda hot watching her get up in Christina's face. Quickly glancing around the room, I noticed no one was paying attention to us, except Phil and Bryce. The latter making his way through the crowd.

Anya lunged at Christina, but I grabbed her around the waist. "Not here, sweetheart. I don't want you to get in trouble for putting your hands on her."

Squirming out of my arms, she turned around and glared at me. "How could you, Hunter?"

"I didn't. If you'd calm the fuck down, you'd realize I would never touch another woman now that I'm with you." I took a deep breath, rubbing a hand down my face. This night was going to hell in a fucking handbasket. "I would never betray you like that."

She lifted one hand and wiped it under her eyes, removing the tears that fell. "Let's get out of here, Carrie. I'm ready to go home."

"No, Anya. We have plans."

"You're such an asshole, Hunter," her friend piped in just as Bryce reached us.

Bryce glanced at Christina walking over to Phil. "What did I miss?"

"No wonder the two of you are friends. Birds of a feather flock together," Carrie spat in his direction.

I'd been so focused on Anya; I didn't even see Carrie standing there. "Carrie," I acknowledged. "It's nice to see you."

"Nope. Don't be nice to me now. You're an asshole, Hunter. I knew you were all the same. I'm just glad Anya found out who you really are before things went too far."

"Carrie, don't call him that," Anya interjected. "Listen, let's just go home."

"If you leave, I'm going to follow you," I said. Our dinner plans were ruined, but we could go out to eat another time. Right now, convincing Anya that I would never be unfaithful to her was my main priority.

"Do whatever you want. I'm leaving." Grabbing Carrie's hand, she pulled her friend behind her as they made their way to the exit. After taking a few steps, she turned back to me.

"Before you arrive on my doorstep, make sure you take the time to decide what you really want before you show up. And let me warn you now, the time for playing games is over. Either you're all in, or you're out. There is no in-between with me. I've warned you once. This time it's a promise. I will walk away from you and never look back. You can count on that." With those parting words, I watched her leave. There was no doubt I'd be following her because I was never giving her up.

"Well, fuck, man. What was that all about?" Bryce stood in front of me. His smile was nonexistent. The look in his eyes was serious.

"Phil and Christina. They set me up." I could hear the frustration in my voice. "This was his way of getting back at me for choking his sorry ass. They planned this entire scenario. Fuck!"

"What are you going to do?"

Glancing over to the last place I saw Phil, I noticed the spot was empty. Good. If I'd seen him still standing there with that smug look on his face, I wouldn't have been responsible for my actions. "I'm going to follow my woman and fuck her until she admits she loves me. Then I'm going to ruin Phil and Christina. They'll regret the day they decided to fuck with me and mine.

A smile lit up Bryce's face. "I hope you'll be ready to admit the same to her."

"Don't worry about me. I got this covered. I'll talk to you later."

"I don't envy you one bit. Good luck with your woman."

Clapping him once on the back, I made my way out of the bar and to the garage. Once I got in my car, I made some phone calls. As soon as the person I was calling picked up on the other end, I set things into motion.

"Hey, Conall. I need a favor. Actually, make that two...."

Once my call with him was finished, I made another call. I meant what I'd said about Phil and Christina. Their jealousy caused Anya to doubt me and my feelings for her. They would pay for their stupidity.

As I made my way to Anya's, I held onto my belief that she'd figured out I was telling the truth about what happened. That had to be why she didn't tell me to go fuck myself when I said I would follow her. She just needed some breathing room. That was fine with me. A few minutes of space was good, but that's all she would get. After tonight, there would never be space between us again.

If tonight proved anything to me, it was that she was the one for me. There was no one else who could take her place. Even in the short time we'd been together, my mind and heart were in one accord.

My bachelor days were over. I was going to marry Anya.

Twenty-Three
Hunter

As soon as I parked and exited my vehicle, Anya's front door opened. For just a moment, her silhouette stood in shadow before she moved. Everything inside of me wanted to run toward the door, but I slowed my pace. I'd been thinking about what I'd say to her this entire time, but none of the words running through my head seemed to work.

They weren't enough.

They didn't feel right.

It was important for Anya to know the real me.

I stopped in my tracks as that thought entered my head. I'd been hiding shit from her since we first met. That's how we got into this situation in the first place. There were things she didn't need to concern herself with, but now I know what I need to do. If there was any chance for me to fix this situation, I needed to be honest with her.

All in or all out. There was no more in-between.

Feeling my phone buzz, I paused to look at the message.

C: All things in motion.

I couldn't help the smile that came over my face. Conall was a good friend and an even better ally to have in my corner. I'd have to make sure Anya and I had dinner with Conall and his wife, Tatiana, very soon. Since I was determined to make her my wife, I wanted her to have some friends in my world. Tatiana was born and bred in this area, and she was good people. It would be good for her and Anya to meet.

Stepping over the threshold, I was waiting for Malachi to come running over to me, but remembered he stayed over with Anya's parents for the night. "Anya, baby?" I called out into the quiet room.

She walked from the back of the house. "Hey. Can you lock the door?"

That was already done, so I didn't bother answering. "I have dinner on the way."

Shaking her head at me, she walked into the living room and sat on the couch. "I'm not hungry." She was wearing different clothes than when I saw her earlier. Shorts and a t-shirt had replaced the sexy black dress and heels she'd been sporting earlier.

"Doesn't matter. Dinner will be here in twenty minutes." Sitting down next to her, I stretched my legs out on the couch. She said nothing for five minutes as I waited for her to speak. To say something. Anything. Curse me out. Call me an asshole. A low laugh came from her as she curled her legs underneath her.

"You think you always have the answers, don't you?"

This was a trick question, right? Funny thing was, I always knew the right thing to say in a business negotiation or in the boardroom. With Anya, I questioned myself all the time. Was I doing the right thing? Saying the right words? Showing her with my actions how much I cared for her. Glancing at her, I knew she was waiting for me to answer.

"No, I don't. Sometimes I worry that I'm not saying the right thing when all I want to do is tell how beautiful you are to me. Or how much I enjoy spending time with you and Malachi?" I reached over to cradle her face in the palm of my hand. "That every day I wake up here with you is a good day for me. No, sweetheart, I don't have all the answers. I just try to do my best to give you what you need because I want to make you happy." Pulling away from me, she sat back against one arm of the couch. She crossed her arms over her stomach, giving me the impression that she was shielding herself from me. A protective gesture that made the organ beating in my chest ache.

"Do you think I'm happy right now, Hunter?"

Another fucking trick question. "I think you're disappointed."

"Wrong. I'm fucking pissed."

I nodded. "That was my next guess." I couldn't stop touching her. One of my hands reached over and rubbed the soft skin of her thigh.

"Stop doing that," she grumbled.

"Stop doing what?" Because if she wanted me to stop touching her, I wasn't sure I could.

"Being so damn agreeable," she sighed. "I gave you an ultimatum at the bar, and you showed up anyway."

"Yeah, I'm here," because there was no other choice. Anya was my future, and I wasn't giving her up. "Was there any question that I'd show up?"

Anya was silent for a long moment, and I can admit it unnerved me. "To be honest, yes. We've had this talk before. Honestly, I don't want to go through all that again. But yeah, there was a part of me that wondered if you'd rethink our relationship."

"Never," I growled. "Come here, baby," I said, grabbing her hand and pulling her toward me. That she didn't give me any resistance told me more than her words could. Placing her ass on my lap, my arms wrapped around her as I pressed my forehead to hers.

I had to think about how I'd feel if I walked into a room and saw another man with his arms around her. To be honest, I probably would have broken his neck and carried her out of the room in my arms. Dropping my head, the feeling that came over me was more visceral than I expected. "I'm sorry." She nodded. Then I heard the sniffles. The wetness flowing down her face was next. "Baby, I would never do that to you. You mean too much to me. You're the only woman I think about. When I'm not working, I want to be with you and Malachi. This past week, sleeping here with you each night has been the first time in a long time that I've had some real fucking peace at night. I would never mess that up."

"You hurt me," she whispered. "You can't imagine how I felt when I saw her kissing you."

I sighed. "Do you believe me when I tell you I wasn't kissing her?"

She nodded. "Yes. Once I thought about it, I realized you weren't holding her, and your eyes were open. Plus, she seemed a little too willing for you to disrespect her in front of me. If you were really involved with her, like we are, she would have put up much more of a fuss."

"Baby, you can guarantee I would never kiss another woman after being with you," I said, kissing her softly on the forehead. "After being in your arms, there's no one else that could make me feel as good as you."

"Who was she?"

Discussing Christina wasn't what I wanted to do right now. "She's someone I used to know."

Anya looked into my eyes. "No, Hunter, you don't get to brush this off. Based on tonight, she's someone you know right now. She made a point to kiss you, to taunt me, to make me break things off with you. So, it's time for you to tell me the whole story."

Leaning my head back on the seat cushion, I briefly shut my eyes before looking at her again.

"Whatever you tell me, it's okay. I know you're with me. All in or all out, right?"

I nodded. "All in." Starting at the beginning, I told her about my night with Christina, how I caught her trying to leave something in my apartment, and how I kicked her out. Then the attempts to see me and reconnect, and finally, finding out Christina and Phil were dating.

"Wait? Did you say Phil? Your neighbor Phil?"

The way she asked the question had me tightening my hold on her. "Yes, my neighbor Phil."

"He approached me tonight while we were at the bar. He was acting odd, as if stalling me. When I shook his hand, he held on for longer than normal. He just made me uncomfortable. Wait a minute. Are you telling me those two were in this together? Why are they so focused on you?"

"I don't know, and I don't care. Let me worry about those two. I can promise they won't be an issue for you after tonight."

She ran her fingers through my hair, removing the band keeping my hair bound. "Don't do anything crazy. I don't want you to get into any trouble. Let's just consider this a minor hiccup in our story. Plus, I don't like being mad at you."

"Sweetheart, I don't like you being mad at me either." Just then, the doorbell rang. "That must be dinner." Lifting her from my lap, I placed her on the other couch cushion and stood to answer the door.

"What did you get?"

Opening the front door, I saw the delivery person standing out front. "Thanks. Please let your boss know I appreciate the special service." Closing the door, I turned around with the bag in hand.

"You had Ocean Prime delivered?" Anya squealed behind me. "I'm so happy because I'm starving."

Walking into the kitchen, I placed the food on the counter before turning to her. "I thought you'd lost your appetite?" At least that's what she said as she walked away from me earlier tonight.

Peeking into the bags, she hummed and yummed as she inhaled. "That was before. When I was angry. Now that we've made up and I don't have to beat up your other woman, my appetite has returned."

Grabbing her around the waist, I pulled her against me. Nipping the skin on her neck, I kissed the spot as she moaned, pressing her ass against my burgeoning length. "You'll never have to worry about another woman. I have you. Trust me, baby, you're all I need."

"And you'd better never forget it," she said with a whimper. "If you don't stop, we'll never eat dinner."

I chuckled. "Oh, sweetheart. I'm going to eat my dinner no matter what. I just have to decide if I'm going to have you as my appetizer or my dessert."

"Appetizer." Her voice was low and husky, filled with need. "Definitely the appetizer."

Turning her around, I lifted her body as she wrapped her legs around my waist. "Your wish is my command." The food could wait. It would be cold by the time we finished, but that's what microwaves were for. I walked us back to her bedroom and lay her down on the mattress. "Don't ever walk away from me again. It hurt me to watch you leave me in anger."

"Don't break my heart again and I won't. You said I was yours and I know you're already mine. We're in this together."

"Yes, baby, we sure are," I said, leaning down to kiss her soft lips. Grabbing her shorts, I pulled them down her body. We spent the next few minutes undressing each other, kissing, touching, and whispering soft words of promise.

Sinking inside her felt like coming home. It didn't matter than I was with her this morning. Didn't matter that we'd been together almost every day for weeks. My battered and bruised heart was safe with this woman, with her and her son. When I first saw her, I had no idea Anya would change my life. Hell, she probably wasn't even trying. Fun was the name of the game until she burrowed herself under my skin. Before she came into my world and made me want more than I ever imagined.

"I love you, Anya."

She looked up at me, and her eyes filled with tears. Cradling my face with her hands, she nodded. "I love you, Hunter."

My breath released in a long exhale. I didn't realize I was nervous about Anya's response until I heard the words.

"I'll never stop wanting you," I said, grabbing her legs and wrapping them around my waist.

"I'll never stop needing you," she responded.

My thrusts became stronger. Harder. I wanted her moans. I needed her screams of pleasure. I wanted her to never let me go.

***

An hour later, I held Anya wrapped in my arms as her body lay on top of mine. "Thank you, baby." Her hand rubbed my chest, the soft touch against my bare skin relaxing me as we recovered from our lovemaking.

"Why are you thanking me?"

"Because you didn't walk away when you could have. You could have believed I'd betrayed you."

She sighed before lifting her face and kissing me along the chin. "I trusted you. Call it a gut feeling or whatever, but I trust you."

I couldn't help the smile that came over my face. "It's because you love me."

She laughed. "Well, you are kinda cute." Just then, her stomach growled.

Shifting our bodies, I kissed her on the top of her head. "Stay here. I'm going to warm up the food for you."

"I can help," she said.

"No, let me take care of you." I pulled on my underwear and exited the room. Something so simple was also the most powerful.

Warming up some of the food, I returned to my woman. I don't know what the future holds, but I know it involves the beautiful woman in front of me. Placing the plate on her lap, I leaned over to kiss her. "Eat. Then it's time for dessert."

"Oh, damn," she squeaked before shoveling food into her mouth.

Epilogue

Anya

3 Months Later...

Watching my son run around the backyard with all the other kids warmed my heart. So much has happened in the last three months, I almost couldn't believe this was my life. Glancing over at Hunter talking with Conall and Bryce, a huge smile covered my face. My man had not been just talking that night when he came to my house after the flare-up at Bachelor Tower. He maintained his apartment for a while, but he never stayed there again. Within a week, his clothes were at my house.

Only a week later, we started looking for a larger place for the three of us. Well, rubbing my stomach...for the four of us.

"Hey, girl," Tatiana came over to me, bumping me with her hip. "Why are you standing over here all by yourself giving your man gaga eyes?"

Laughing, I nodded. "I can't help it. My man is fine."

"Girl, you ain't never lied. Then again, I only have eyes for one man, which he knows. But he'd still be a little perturbed if he caught me staring at your Viking."

"Um, that Italian Stallion of yours? He ain't got nothing to worry about. Shit, I think we're both lucky as hell." We gave each other a high-five, sipping on juice as we stared across the yard.

After Hunter and I turned the corner with our relationship, he'd introduced me to his friend Conall and his wife, Tatiana. I wasn't naïve. I knew the name O'Shea. You can't be in Boston for any length of time and not know who Conall O'Shea was. When I first met him, something about his eyes made me take a step back. There was darkness hiding beneath his gaze, but then something shifted, he smiled, and the look was gone. I'd never forget it, but I also realized he and Hunter had a similar style. They looked at people as if they were looking at their souls.

As he was talking on the phone with Conall, I walked up behind him. I heard the words, *Phil and Christina and handled*. I was a smart woman, so you know what I did? I turned my ass around and went in the other direction. I loved my man, but I'd come to understand that he was no angel. He was definitely living up to his name. As long as he kept that side of himself away from me, Malachi, and our new baby, then I was okay with it.

I watched Hunter break away from the other two men and make his way over to me. Admiring his form, I thanked my lucky stars every day that Carrie forced me to go out that night. Without that push, I never would have met the man of my dreams, the man who gave me the gift of another child, and who placed a four-karat diamond on my finger.

"I'm gonna go check on my husband," Tatiana said with a smile. "Hey, Hunter. Having fun?"

"Always," he responded, tipping his drink at her as she walked away. Once he made it in front of me, he stopped. "Hey, sweetheart. How are you feeling?" Ever since I'd told him I was pregnant, he's been super attentive. Which was almost impossible since the man was already a little obsessive about me. He'd finally convinced me to stop working at the law firm once I hit the six-month mark in my pregnancy. I was still trying to decide if it was worth trying to convince him that I wanted to go back to work once I gave birth. That was a decision for another time and not something I needed to worry about right now.

"I'm feeling great. Are you ever going to stop hovering?"

"Never," he smirked at me.

"I've done this before," I said, motioning over to Malachi, who hadn't stopped playing since we'd arrived.

He nodded. "I know, but I wasn't there with you when you were pregnant with Malachi. But I'm here now, and I want to make sure I do this right."

"I love you, Hunter."

The smile that came over his face at my words made my heart full. He always seemed so amazed whenever I said the words to him. Learning more about his past, I understood why. We were leaving next week to go visit his mom. According to her, she couldn't wait to meet her first grandchild, Malachi, and already had so many things lined up for them.

"I love you, future Mrs. Malone."

Hugging him around his waist, I rested my head on his chest. "You like saying that, don't you?"

"Baby, I'll say it every day until it becomes a reality."

"Just one more month," I responded. One thing Hunter would not budge on was that he wanted to be married before our baby was born. In response, I told him I didn't want to be nine months pregnant and standing at the altar. We negotiated so that we both got what we wanted. My only caveat was that my parents and his mother had to be with us to celebrate our union. "Do you ever regret giving up the bachelor life?"

"Not for one second. Having you and Malachi mean everything to me. We're creating a family of our own. We're building a future," he said, stepping closer and cradling my face within one palm. "I could never regret that life. How could I miss what was essentially a half-life? I wasn't really living until I met you."

"Mommy! Daddy!" Malachi yelled out as he ran in our direction. About one month ago, Malachi walked into the living room and over to Hunter and blurted out, "Daddy, can we go to the park?" I think both of us were floored by his words. Before I could speak one word, Hunter replied. "Absolutely, buddy. Let's eat breakfast and get dressed." From that day forward, Hunter was his daddy. Since Malachi's father only paid child support but had no contact with him, we took steps to have Hunter adopt Malachi.

Watching Hunter pick up our little boy, I could feel the tears in my eyes. There was so much ahead of us. But together, we were ready for everything the world would throw our way. As long as I had Hunter by my side, I knew life would be a beautiful adventure.

~ FIN ~

Thank You!

Thank you for supporting my writing. It truly means a lot to me. If you enjoyed Ruthless Bachelor, Hunter and Anya's story, please take a few moments to leave a review on the platform where this book was purchased.

As you may know, reviews help motivate authors as we continue writing and bringing you great stories. The more reviews on a book, the more visible it becomes to other readers.

Thank you for your support!

* * * * *

Keep swiping to read an excerpt from **<u>Secret Devotion</u>**.

Secret Devotion
Summary

A love so pure, it's lasted more than twenty years.

For years, Tanner Scott and Chantell Warren fought to keep their love alive, while also hiding their relationship from the world around them. Now, just as things are about to change for the better, everything's falling apart. Family expectations and long-held secrets were bubbling up to the surface and drowning them both beneath the waves, raising long-held doubts and unanswered questions about the strength of their love.

Tanner loved Chantell and would gladly tell the world. If only his father hadn't threatened to cut him out of his inheritance.

Chantell would give everything she had in this world to be at Tanner's side. If only her parents weren't so disappointed in her life choices.

How could Tanner and Chantell survive a lifetime together, when they couldn't see their way past the world threatening to tear them apart?

One
Tanner

Looking down at the woman lying in bed next to him as she shifted on the mattress, Tanner Scott smiled softly as she mumbled in her sleep. Yeah, he'd worn her ass out and loved her so damn good, he put her ass to sleep.

Then again, she'd put it on him just as good and he pulled her body closer to his as he lay there reflecting on how this night would end. He wanted to wake her up so he could feel her body writhe in passion for him. Taking a deep breath, he smiled at the thought of her voice, raspy from her screaming his name. Her tight, curvy body fit his perfectly. He'd always known she was made for him. One long finger traced her lips, and he thickened at the remembered feel of her kissing his naked flesh.

His deep love for her was expressed in their whispered conversations as they lay in each other's arms. Every kiss she bestowed on him to seal her words of love. Stolen moments with only the two of them are what he lived for. When they were alone, and the outside world was shut out, those were the times he felt truly alive.

When no one else was around to question their love or how they felt about each other, was pure fucking bliss. These private moments were the only time they could express just how deeply they felt for each other. Chantell was his entire world. His everything.

If only he'd shared his feelings about her with his family. His friends.

For twenty years, he'd loved her more than he'd loved himself.

And for every one of those years, he'd hidden his love for her from the world.

For that sin against his woman, he knew he'd have to pay the price one day soon. But that day was not today. Some would call him selfish. Others may call him an asshole. If Chantell called him hers, the other names meant nothing.

Tanner looked down into Chantell's beautiful face and he knew no matter what happened before this moment, or what they had to deal with in the future, there was no way in hell he'd give her up.

He'd been playing a dangerous game for a while now and time was up. His need to keep her close outweighed any reservations he had about keeping their relationship quiet.

Briefly closing his eyes, he thought about how they'd gotten to this point. The things he'd done, and would still do, made him cringe. He'd be more disgusted with his behavior if the benefit of having Chantell in his arms didn't feel so damn good.

In his quest to gain revenge against his father, he'd asked her to hide away as if he were ashamed of her. He wasn't. She was his greatest joy and the one person who could give him peace. But Tanner knew he'd asked too much of her. Yet, she gave willingly whenever he asked. Exhaling slowly, he was coming to a decision and that shit didn't feel right at all.

It was time they stopped hiding.

The things he'd asked her to do were beneath him and they both knew it. Sneaking around. Going out on dates where no one they knew would see them. Showing up at her home only after the sun had gone down, and stars blanketed the dark skies.

He thought of the sadness reflected in her eyes when he'd arrived tonight under the cover of darkness. Her eyes told him she was at her limit. That this couldn't go on this way much longer.

Hurt and shame began to fill him as he took in the irony of their situation. But at the time they'd started down this path, there'd been no other way. Or at least, that's what he'd told himself at the time.

Tanner knew his behavior wasn't fair to Chantell, but his need for her was too great. Nothing could pull him away from her and he'd dare anyone to try. Hiding in plain sight wasn't how he'd planned for them to live their lives together, but this was where they were. At least for a little while longer.

There were many times she'd tried to break it off with him, but he wasn't having that shit. She knew it, too. On the occasions when she did try to pull that mess and break it off with him, he shut it down quick. Leaving him wasn't something he'd willingly accept. Hell, he wouldn't accept that shit under any circumstances.

The woman lying next to him has been part of his life for so long, he knew surviving without her by his side was not possible. Not now. Not ever. Chantell was the other half of his twisted, imperfect soul.

Frustrated with the direction of his thoughts, he rubbed a hand down his face to clear his thoughts. With his past reactions to her requests to break things off, how would he explain his actions at the end of the night?

His friend Jason, the only one who knew about Tanner and Chantell's relationship, told him he was going about this the wrong way. He'd warned Tanner that he was going to break her heart for good. That he was risking their relationship and making decisions without involving the other person. Tanner knew his friend meant well but no way would happen. She loved him too much to simply walk away.

All he needed was a little more time to make things right. Chantell knew this better than he did. Chantell would understand once he explained what had to be done. They'd been together so long; she could almost read his mind. Over the years, she'd come to know what he was thinking before he got the words out. There was no way she'd ever fault him for doing what was best for them.

Then again, sometimes his baby just got so wrapped up in her dreams of their future, she forgot what was most important. When his twenty-eighth birthday hit, life would change for them. He'd finally have what he needed to build something real for them, without his father hanging over their heads.

Once he had access to his trust fund, they could live their life without worry. Move to another city and start over. He just needed more time. Six more months. It was a blip on the radar compared to twenty years of being by each other's side.

And until the time came when he could take his woman and leave this backward town behind him, he was right where he wanted to be. With his woman's warm, enticing body next to him, ready to accept him into her body as he made love to her all night. There was no feeling in the world like her warm sheath welcoming him home. Being with her like that was how he wanted to end every day.

Over the years, he'd become addicted to her special brand of love. Unless he got to lay between her beautiful brown legs and stroke inside her body until they both moaned out an orgasm, he couldn't sleep at night. Her sensual sounds when they made love were his evening lullabies and she rocked him to sleep every damn night. Hands so soft, they felt like satin on his skin, would rub the tension from his shoulders as they sat cocooned in their private bubble. Nothing could compare to what he had right here.

As he lay there thinking about their relationship, he could finally admit to himself that he'd asked more from her than he should have. And she'd loved him enough to give him everything he needed.

Every time.

Without question.

Even when she didn't want to.

When they were in their first year of college, their relationship changed from best friends to lovers and his world had flipped on its head. They both understood being together wouldn't be easy. If they wanted to be together, they'd have to fight for it.

It was Chantell who'd convinced him to give them a chance. To not worry about what others thought or how they felt about their relationship. Back then, she'd been strong enough to take anything and fight any battle. Now, years later, her strength and commitment to him—to them—made him love her even more.

But after eight years of being together, even he could feel something changing inside her. He'd taken too long to fix this situation and now he was stuck between a rock and a hard place. The thought of asking her to take on anymore, to deal with more bullshit, made him sick to his stomach. He knew the time was coming when she'd begin to question his love for her. His commitment to their relationship. His ability to keep his promises.

Although she'd turned her face away from him when he'd arrived tonight, he'd seen the tears in her eyes. He'd be damned if he allowed her to leave him though. Not after all this time. They were too close to the endgame.

He'd watched the hurt grow in her eyes each time he prepared to leave each morning before the sun came up. It all boiled down to one question. The one he dreaded hearing each night, even though he knew there was no hiding from it.

If you love me as much as I love you, how can you keep me hidden away like I'm your dirty little secret?

Lately, each time she asked, his answer was simply inadequate. He knew the more he asked her to just give him time, the more reason she had to doubt his words. Doubt him. He'd been treading on thin ice for a while and tonight he feared it was going to break underneath him.

*****

Secret Devotion is Now Available in both ebook and Print.

About the Author

USA Today bestselling author Reana Malori pens gripping multicultural/interracial contemporary romance novels full of love, steam, and suspense that will pull you into her world. You'll want to run away with these smoking hot book boyfriends and find a happily ever after alongside heroines you'd love as a best friend. Grab a glass of wine and enjoy!

Reana began her writing journey in 2009, releasing her first novella, To Love a Marine. Since then, she has published more than 40 books, to include Weekend Fling, Finding Faith, Odin's Honor, and Secret Devotion. She currently resides in Montclair, Virginia with her husband and two sons who keep her busy laughing, having fun, and making sure she doesn't take herself too seriously.

Love and Hugs,
Reana Malori ♥

Also by Reana Malori
****

Made in the USA
Middletown, DE
29 August 2023

37348925R00224